MAKE A WISH
& *Blow*

Christina James

Make A Wish and Blow

Published by Valerie Harris
Copyright 2012 by Valerie Harris
Cover by Angela Anderson, Angela Anderson Design
ISBN: 978-1-938799-02-0

Previously published by The Wild Rose Press under *Make A Wish and Blow by Christina James.*

Interior Layout by www.formatting4U.com

Dedication

To my children, Courtney and Scott Jr., for all the nights they gave me my space and the time to write.

Chapter One

Turning another year older wasn't the highlight of Cassandra Wright's day. Being a horny single woman just added to her misery. She sat at her kitchen table sipping the glass of wine she'd poured as soon as she arrived home from work. She ignored the four voice mail messages from various friends wanting to get together to celebrate her birthday. Oh sure, she enjoyed partying, dancing, and having a great time as much as the next person, but none of that mattered as she held a private pity party in her tiny kitchen. The man she desperately loved had apparently forgotten her birthday.

When her doorbell rang, she cringed, knowing one of her friends had decided to come by and haul her out on the town. If she believed they'd go away, she'd ignore the ding-dong sound. But she knew better. With her car in the driveway during a humid Connecticut summer evening, it was obvious she was home and, unless she wanted to continue to listen to the shrill ringing, she'd better answer the door. She prayed they wouldn't sing a pathetic rendition of Happy Birthday. She gently placed the wine glass on her counter before walking to the front door.

When she peeked through the view hole, she

immediately perked up, recognizing Daren Hughes, her best friend since sixth grade. So he hadn't forgotten her birthday after all! Daren was also, to her utter disappointment and constant torture, her *platonic* friend.

Cassandra opened the door and quickly ran her gaze over the hard male body leaning against the doorframe. At twenty-nine, Daren was six-feet-two with chocolate brown eyes and thick wavy hair the color of caramel. His body was toned and lean, without an ounce of fat anywhere, thanks to his relentless daily workout regimen. The solid muscles of his thighs strained against the light blue material of his jeans. Broad arms and flat abs were covered by a tight short sleeve black T-shirt. Daren made her mouth water and her pussy clench every time she set eyes on him. What she wouldn't give to nibble on him for one damn night. She could easily picture her teeth nibbling along that hard skin inch by inch, tasting the saltiness of flesh that was firm and muscular. She'd start her feasting along the curve of his thick neck and head down to…well…anywhere on his body would be fine with her.

Cassandra spoke softly, squashing the urge to fan herself. "If you start singing to me, I'll slam the door and not talk to you for a week."

"You'd break my heart, babe," Daren replied easily, his deep voice lulling her into a hornier state. He held a lovely bouquet of red roses and a small ice cream cake. "Besides, the only singing I do is in the shower. You'd have to join me, if you're interested in how well I carry a tune. I promise you won't be disappointed."

His smile was devastating as it widened to show perfect teeth, the kind also made for nibbling heated skin. Her body heated a few degrees at the thought of his teeth grazing lazily over her hot flesh. God, how she wanted to take that shower. If only he was serious and not teasing her like he usually enjoyed doing, she'd strip now and haul him into the bathroom. Just the thought made her panties dampen with arousal. Her legs shifted in response and her pussy heated up. If she could only clench her thighs together hard enough, then maybe her cunt wouldn't be so aware of Daren's body inches from hers. She hated how easily he could arouse her with just one look, one word, one touch.

She leaned her shoulder on the open door for support. "Tell me, Daren, did you stop by to flirt or did you have something else on your mind?"

Shrugging, he kept his eyes on her. "Wanted to wish you a happy birthday."

She sighed. "It's just another day."

"No, it's your special day. You should be celebrating, especially since it's Friday."

She leaned her head against the door. "Only kids celebrate birthdays. Adults really have no right. It only signifies another year of leaving youth behind."

He frowned. "Ah, I can see the Cynical Cass is here tonight. Pity, since I much prefer the Playful Cass."

If only she could tell him about all the games she'd like to play with him between her 1200-thread count soft-as-heaven bed sheets. Oh, the hell with that. She'd play games with him on the cold hard floor if it meant that magnificent body was pressing hers into the gleaming wood planks. But his friendship was more

3

important than a few orgasms—no matter how glorious they'd be.

"Not cynical. Just worn out. That's all." *I'm exhausted from facing the fact I can't have you.*

"Uh-huh." He sounded doubtful. Of course he wouldn't believe her. She'd never been able to lie to him.

She prayed he wouldn't interrogate her now. If he did, there was a good chance she'd jump into his arms and spill her heart.

"You gonna invite me in?"

"Oh God, yes. I'm sorry. Told you I was tired." She stepped aside and let him move past before shutting the door.

He placed the cake on the foyer table in her front hall and faced her. His massive body hovered over her, making her feel shorter than her five-foot-four stature, and then pinned her against the closed door.

"No problem," he said, leaning on his elbow and pushing into her personal space. Now he looked straight down into her eyes as she tilted her head back to keep eye contact.

"In answer to your question, I came over to spend the night with my favorite girl. Well, that is unless she has other plans." His finger skimmed her cheek. She sucked in her breath.

She laughed hoping it didn't sound nervous. "Favorite girl, my ass. You have more girls than you can keep straight."

His face remained serious. "Hey, that may be true, sweetie, but none of them compare to you. You're my favorite. So what do you say? You going to let me make the night memorable for you?"

She raised her eyebrow. "Memorable, huh? Now you've got my attention."

He smiled. "I bet I do. And you've got mine. The night is yours. What do you want to do?"

Fuck you, then fuck you again.

She looked past his body to where he left the ice cream cake. "Looks like we should start with dessert first, before it melts, then get something for dinner."

His thigh brushed hers as he turned to glance at the cake then faced her again. The firm touch of his muscle against the bare skin under her skirt heated her flesh. A slow, warm tingle traveled up her thigh to pool in her belly. The warmth was like the slow stroking of a flame, every cell in her body aware of his closeness. Every cell longed for his touch. Even her brain wasn't immune as she struggled to keep focused on the connection. Just a slight shift of his feet and they no longer touched. With the connection lost, disappointment filled her.

"Sounds good," he said, simply.

She blew out an aggravated breath. She was practically humping his friggin' leg. What the hell had gotten into her tonight? Why was she acting like a schoolgirl instead of a grown woman? She rationalized that any breathing woman would react to such a sexy male body. It was all just a normal female-male reaction and nothing to do with the fact that each night she dreamt of his hot, sweaty body gliding over hers in every position imaginable. And now the subject of those dreams was standing oh so close to her.

She quickly snapped back to reality. "Thank you for the roses, Daren. I can smell them all the way over here."

"Mmmmm. I can only smell you, Cass." His head bent, his nose lightly resting behind her ear. When he inhaled, his warm breath teased her ear. She expected her legs to drop from under her. "Of course, you always smell great. Makes a man want to lay you down and kiss you from head to toe. You're intoxicating, Cass." His whispered words created goosebumps over her entire body.

Her mouth opened in shock. It took her a minute to find her voice. "Daren?"

He slowly pulled his head back, but remained nose to nose with her. She swallowed hard, her mouth suddenly so dry. He said nothing. His gaze scanned her face before fixating on her eyes. Was that lust in the brown depths staring back at her?

"Daren? Do you have a head injury or something?"

"No, babe. Why?"

This close, Cassandra could see the creases around his eyes when he frowned.

"Because it sounds like you're hitting on me. That thing you just did to my ear…"

"Thing?" he asked, his lips forming a sexy smirk.

"Oh, shut up. You know what I mean." She shoved against him, but he didn't budge. "You practically stuck your tongue in my ear."

"Mmmmm. Now that sounds like fun."

What? Oh God, Daren had obviously encountered extraterrestrials, because she was not his type and yet he was clearly hitting on her. Hadn't she dreamt of this moment? But now that it was happening, it seemed so surreal.

"What's gotten into you?" she demanded, her back

6

against the door and her eyes mesmerized by his.

He smiled again, his eyes offering a challenge. "Tell me to stop and I will."

Stop? Was he fucking crazy? This was the closest he'd been to her other than on a dance floor, and he'd never pulled these moves on her there. Oh, hell no, she didn't want it to stop.

She smiled, her heart did a slow drum roll. "So is this why you came over? To tease me? Doesn't sound like a very nice thing to do to your best friend."

"It's not a very nice thing to do to myself either."

"What are you talking about?"

His gaze flicked down to his waist then back to hers. "I think if you lowered those gorgeous eyes of yours south of my belt, you'd see that you've given me a hard-on with no relief in sight."

Okay, she'd just *look*, but only to satisfy her curiosity. And she didn't care about any damn superstitions about curiosity and cats. She was a woman. Her eyes widened at the obvious erection straining against the front of his jeans. The thickness grew longer as she watched and she swore it flexed. Well, now she knew what curiosity did to her *pussy*…it flooded instantly with desire.

"*I* gave *you* that? You're the one who has me pinned against the damn door, practically sucking on my neck."

"I hardly have you pinned, Cass. You could move away at any time." He leaned in again, his lips against her ear. "But make it soon before I change my mind about letting you get away. Maybe I like to have you pinned as you call it."

She took a long steadying breath, closing her eyes

briefly, then opening them to see that he was still there. "So this is what you came here for? To play games?"

"Do you really want to know why I came here tonight, Cass?"

"I've only asked like five times."

A long finger brushed a curly strand of hair behind her ear. "I wanted to see you. Wanted to make your birthday special." His voice dropped to barely louder than a whisper. "And, of course, you need your birthday spanking."

For a long moment, Cassandra could only stare at her handsome best friend, the vision of him spanking her the only thought in her mind. His words, his stare, entranced her.

"Promises, promises," she muttered, not really meaning to say it out loud, but it was too late. The words had slipped passed her lips.

The gleam of Daren's eyes told Cassandra he wasn't kidding.

"Are you serious?" she asked, her voice giving away her shock followed by a nervous giggle.

He continued looking down at her. "Absolutely. You know better than anyone that once I set my mind to something, I finish it."

She swallowed hard and told herself to breathe. She wanted to speak, but her voice was mute. When she opened her mouth to take a deep breath, words slowly formed. "And you know better than anyone that I don't play games, Daren. So stop. We'd better eat that ice cream cake before it melts everywhere."

She pushed easily past, his muscular body giving way. She walked the few feet to the table and picked up the box and flowers. Daren's hard body pressed against her, his chest to her back.

His voice whispered into her ear. "I'm not into playing games either, Cass, unless, of course, they include sex toys and paddles. You take life too serious. I'm here to show you how to have a little fun."

She turned to face him, her bundles getting squished between their bodies when he didn't move back even an inch. "I know how to have fun, Daren. Let's start with this cake, then you're taking me dancing."

He followed her into the kitchen and leaned against the counter while she busied herself with plates, forks, and a knife.

His hand clasped over hers when she went to slice the cake. "Uh-huh, Cass. Not so fast."

"It's melting. If we wait any longer it'll be soup."

He stood behind her. His arms circled her until his hands covered hers as she held the knife over the cake. His mouth rested on her ear. Every cell in her body was alive with the awareness that he was hard, muscular, and potent. Her pussy wept with little waves of pleasure, pleading for his attention. She did everything she could not to lean her head back onto his chest and offer her throat up for his exploration.

"You need to make a wish, baby. Make it one I can help come true."

The promise in his voice was all she needed to tremble. She swallowed hard, closed her eyes, and formed a thought. There was only one wish she wanted—Daren to be hers, forever. No fling would do. No one-night stand would satisfy. That would leave her aching more than she was now. One taste of Daren would make her want him forever. She knew that as much as she knew she needed air to live.

"Make a wish, Cass. Make a wish," Daren whispered into her ear.

Cassandra silently made her wish, allowing herself a moment to envision it coming true and waking up to Daren every day for the rest of her life. But the Roaming Romeo was not the settling down type. Daren preferred a different woman in his bed every night. He liked to play and enjoyed variety. To him, the thrill was in the chase. Once he got a woman in his bed he tired of her quickly and set his sights on the next target. Cassandra couldn't ever remember when Daren had a steady girlfriend. She had managed to stay in his life all these years simply because she'd never fucked him. Aw hell, didn't he just think of her like he would a sister? She could hear her dreams slowly shatter. If only birthday wishes could become reality.

Cassandra sighed and opened her eyes.

"Gonna tell me what the wish was, Cass?" Daren cooed, still close to her ear.

"No. You know if I tell you then it won't come true."

He laughed and raised his head, but remained with his arms around her. "Or maybe I could make it come true. There's nothing I wouldn't do for you, sweetheart. You know all you have to do is ask."

Would you be mine? Cassandra smiled at the cliché and immediately thought of the little Valentine cards kids traded at school. Daren could never be hers.

But at least she had his friendship. Adding sex to the mix would destroy the one relationship that had remained a constant in her life. Even the best orgasm in the world wasn't worth that, unless there could be future orgasms. Her only future with Daren was as his *platonic* best friend.

"You've brought me cake. That's a start." She avoided eye contact, feeling too vulnerable about her silly wishes.

Daren helped her slice into a cake that was now very creamy. She scooped two pieces onto plates, handed him one, and walked to the kitchen table. He sat next to her, his knee brushing her leg. Why was she so aware of his touch tonight?

She welcomed the coldness from the ice cream. Her body felt as if she'd laid out in the sunshine all day. She prayed her cheeks weren't flushed, although the warmth indicated they were. So she kept her head lowered, hoping the ice cream would cool her down.

"This is delicious. Very creamy," Daren said, his voice hinting of charm she didn't believe was just for silly ice cream. Could it be for her?

Cassandra risked a glance up and wished she hadn't. Daren was licking his spoon, front to back, in slow strokes. Visions of him doing that to her pussy danced in her head.

She spoke softly, her eyes still mesmerized by his tongue. "This was a very nice surprise, Daren. Thank you."

"Pleasure's all mine."

She laughed when a drop of vanilla ice cream smeared onto the corner of his mouth when he took another spoonful. "Eat much? You're wearing it," she teased, placing her spoon carefully on her plate.

She leaned over, a gesture too automatic to think about, and wiped her fingertip across the corner of his mouth to remove the ice cream drop. As fast as a lightening, he captured her hand. She sat in stunned fascination as he raised her finger to his mouth, his firm lips closing over it and taking it into the wet, warmth of his mouth. She gasped when he sucked on her finger with a slow pull so erotic that her pussy spasmed in greedy awareness. Oh my God, his mouth was like heaven—full of promises of out-of-this-world pleasures.

Her eyes shot to his, the chocolate brown color glazed over with lust. His mouth moved slowly over her finger, licking it up then down. His stare was intense, her body reacting in more ways than she could imagine from such a simple touch. Her skin was feverish. Her mind was blank. The smell of vanilla from the cake made her drunk with desire. All she could focus on, all she could see, was Daren's mouth holding her finger prisoner. All she could feel was the heat of his mouth, the pressure of his tongue.

With deliberate slowness, he withdrew her finger from his mouth, kissing the tip before releasing it. He smiled wickedly, the devilish grin acknowledging that he'd turned her on.

"My, with lips like those, it's no wonder you can have any woman you want," Cassandra said, trying to make light of the situation. The last thing she wanted was to confirm the affect he had on her.

"Not true. I don't always get every woman I want."

She laughed and stood to bring her plate to the sink. "Yeah, right. There isn't a woman in this state that hasn't fallen into your bed."

"You haven't," he said matter-of-factly as he brought his plate to the sink and stood beside her.

"Ah, true. But we're best friends, so I don't count."

"On the contrary, my dear, I believe you count a lot."

She stared at him before speaking. She didn't want to be teased right now. "I need to change. You're taking me dancing. So go home, change, and pick me up in an hour."

He smiled, wide and bright. "Aren't you the bossy little thing, huh? But you forget that I like to be in charge."

"Your Dominant side doesn't count with me. I'm your friend not your lover, so dominating me won't happen."

He smiled dangerously, as if she'd just challenged a tiger to a wrestling match. Expecting a smart-ass comeback from him, she was shocked when he said nothing but continued to watch her intensely.

"It's my birthday. I get to call the shots," she continued and walked him by the hand to the door. "One hour."

His hand squeezed hers before letting go. Once in the hall, Daren turned to face her, his eyes dancing with heat. "One hour, Cass, and I'll be back. If you're not ready then we go out the way you are when I get here. Dressed or not. And I choose the place we dance."

His smile was soft but he left no room for argument as he swiftly turned and walked out into the night. Cassandra looked at her watch, noted the time, and smiled. If he thought he could boss her around, he'd better think twice. After all these years, didn't the man know any better? Oh, she would sorely test

Daren's Dominant side if he thought of using it on her.

Daren Hughes would be eating out of her hand by the end of the night not just sucking on her finger.

****

Jesus Christ, what the hell had he been thinking? Daren parked his BMW in the assigned parking spot under his condo complex. Walking to his apartment was uncomfortable to say the least. The massive hard-on he sported, all thanks to Cassandra, bulged in his jeans. Fuck!

He let himself into the apartment, walked to the bathroom, and turned the shower on cold. He stripped, stepped under the stream, and cursed loudly when the frigid water hit his heated body.

Christ, he'd gone over to wish Cassandra a happy birthday, not to seduce her. But the woman made it too easy, looking like a sex kitten with those pouty lips and come-fuck-me brown eyes that darkened to a deep chocolate when she was aroused. Her slender body fit perfectly against his. And that long, gorgeous, dark brown hair flowed down her back in thick waves. He could imagine taking a fistful of those locks to hold her against him as he pounded her pussy from the behind.

He growled loudly and lifted his face to the icy water. He had to stop thinking about Cassandra that way. She was his best friend, his only truly trusted companion. Yeah, she had a body that made his mouth water and his cock harden. But as much as he needed—no wanted—to feel her luscious hips thrusting into his, to feel her slender body writhing under his, he couldn't expose her to his Dominant side.

What he'd expect from Cassandra in bed would be more than their friendship could survive. She'd never accept his dark side, his need to dominate. Hell, it was more than most women could handle as he knew all too painfully well. He didn't get bored with women like Cassandra thought. Instead, women couldn't handle him in bed. Sure, they all talked the talk when they first met him. They all wanted to be dominated, but once he got them into bed and showed them exactly what he meant, they never came back.

Losing Cassandra the same way would be too much to bear. Oh, but the fun he could show her especially once her sarcasm got to work. Yeah, she'd surely challenge the best of his patience. He'd enjoy every second too.

Daren had dressed in record time before realizing he was rushing to get back to Cassandra. Damn. It was going to be a long night if he didn't get his hormones under control. Even if he'd had the time to jerk off, it wouldn't have helped. It wouldn't be the same as Cassandra's hot body riding him and her sweet pussy milking his cock.

The ten-minute drive back to her place took an eternity. Daren backed into a parking spot and strolled up the stairs.

He knocked on Cassandra's door, knowing she wouldn't be ready just because he told her to be. He smiled, his cock flexing in his tan slacks. His Dominant side would love to tame that little vixen. She needed a lifetime of taming and he'd be sure to enjoy it, but that wouldn't happen. His best friend never gave a man a chance in the Forever After Department.

His breath hitched when Cassandra opened her door, dressed in a red skin-hugging dress that barely covered her ass. The neckline gripped her ample cleavage snugly, her nipples proudly perked against the material. Long, silky legs ran on forever above three inch, red stiletto heels. Her long, dark brown hair flowed over her shoulders down her back. His hand wanted so badly to take a fistful of those beautiful long strands and pull her to him. He'd devour the luscious mouth that currently smiled with a feline grin.

"Right on time, Daren. Bet you thought I wouldn't be ready."

"Thought crossed my mind. Remember, Cass. I know you well."

"Mmmmm. We'll see about that. Now where are we going?"

He took her slender hand in his and walked down the stairs to the car. The click of her heels on the cement drew his attention to her gorgeous legs. Immediately, visions of those legs wrapped around his waist had his cock surging to life. He would have her keep those heels on while she rode him. His breath hitched at the thought of Cassandra standing before him, naked, dressed only in those sexy shoes.

He opened the passenger door for her and looked his fill as she seated herself. "A place I frequent often," he told her. "Thought I'd spice things up for you tonight."

Her eyes widened at his words. He shut the door and walked quickly to the driver's side. As soon as he was seated, her scent assaulted him like a solid punch to the gut. She smelled of lilacs and vanilla. To keep from touching her, he immediately put the car in drive and pulled out into traffic.

"When you said a place you frequent, do you mean one of those fetish clubs?"

He glanced at her quickly before returning his eyes to the road. "Yes. It's Club Perform. But it's not what you're thinking."

Her giggle made his blood heat. "Oh? And what do you think I'm thinking?"

He grinned. "You're thinking there will be people chained to the wall getting whipped, or everyone will be dressed in leather." He looked at her. "Am I right?"

She laughed. The soft chuckle tightened his stomach.

"Okay. Half right. I imagined the leather, but not the whipping part. Do they really do that at those clubs?"

Her innocent curiosity shot right to his groin and his erection hardened painfully. God, the last thing he needed was for her to be interested in the erotic lifestyle he embraced. He would love to tutor her in the erotic side of lovemaking, to see her face flushed with passion and her clit swelled with lust.

"Daren! Watch out!"

Daren slammed on the brakes, tires squealing, and stopped inches from the rear end of a police cruiser at a red light.

"Shit!" Daren yelled, watching the blue lights come on in front of him and the two police officers step from their vehicle. "Great."

Daren rolled down the window, praying he didn't have to step out sporting the massive hard-on in his pants.

"Problem with your brakes, sir?" the young officer asked.

"No, sir. I'm sorry. Foot slipped. That's all."

The officer looked into the vehicle at Cassandra

then back to Daren. "Where are you headed?"

"Taking the lady out dancing. It's her birthday."

The cop gave him a shit-eating grin. "Lucky guy. License and registration. Ma'am, I'm going to need you to step out of the vehicle."

"Why? What the hell for?" Daren demanded as he opened his wallet to retrieve his license.

She patted his arm, the simple touch scorching his skin. "It's okay, Daren. Just do what they say."

The other young officer opened the door for Cassandra and offered his hand to help her out while Daren could only sit there. Bastards were infatuated with her. Daren fought against a wave of jealousy he'd never experienced before. Why did they need her to step out of the vehicle other than to ogle her? Hell. He wished they had stayed at her place and he had gone with his original plan and ordered take-out. Then he could've talked her into that birthday spanking. Oh hell, now wasn't the time to think of that.

Daren sat in his car like a caged animal. He wanted to get out and go to Cassandra. He could see her in his rearview mirror speaking with the officer while the other officer sat in the front seat of the cruiser, presumably running his info. Damn! Well, he sure was making Cassandra's birthday memorable, but he wanted to be the only man she remembered, not the two young stud wanna-be's in uniform.

The officer exited the cruiser, but instead of returning to Daren, he walked to the back of the car and started talking with Cassandra. A moment later, her laughter sang through the air.

Daren clenched his fists. What the hell was so funny? And why was she still out there? Surely they'd stared at her long enough. Another peal of laughter. His teeth ground together and his jaw was so taut it ached. She was so getting a spanking when they got home!

"Excuse me, officer? Are we done here?" Daren yelled out the window before mentally counting to ten.

A moment passed before Cassandra walked back to the car, where the officer opened her door and once again offered her a hand as she sat down.

"Thank you, Officer Riley. You're the sweetest thing."

Oh please!

The other officer came to Daren's window. "Pay attention to the road, Mr. Hughes. While I can't blame you for being distracted by such a lovely young woman, you need to focus while driving." He handed him back his paperwork. "Have a nice birthday, Cassandra. Enjoy Club Perform."

"Thank you, Officer Mathews," she said, giving a little wiggle of her fingers and a sinful smile.

When they were finally back on the road, Daren cursed. "What the hell was so damn funny back there?"

"What?" Innocence echoed her words. "Oh, you mean with the officers?"

"No. I mean with the damn boogeyman. Of course I mean with the officers."

She giggled, the sound shot all the way to his cock, making it grow hard again. "Oh my God. Are you jealous, Daren?"

His hands tightened on the steering wheel. "What? Of course not. Why the hell would I be jealous of two cops when I'm the one you're out with?"

"Oh, I don't know. They were really handsome. And muscular. And I am single. They'd be good candidates for me to date."

Daren grunted.

"They were such gentlemen, all concerned about my safety." The whisper in her voice made his cock ache painfully. "They wanted to make sure I was with you willingly."

"What?" His head whipped around to look at her. "Why the hell wouldn't you be?"

Her gaze fluttered between him and the road. "Daren, maybe we should talk when you're not driving."

His gaze flew back to the road. "I can drive and talk, damn it."

Her hand slid over his thigh, soothing up and down. *God, please go higher!* His body tensed, hoping he wouldn't cum in his pants from her touch but damn he wanted to feel that slender hand stroke his cock.

"You're right. I'm with you and not them, so no need to be jealous. They were going to write you a ticket for reckless driving, until I flirted with them and managed to change their minds."

His jaw tensed so much it ached. "I would rather have gotten the ticket than have you out there flirting with them. I can afford a goddamn ticket."

"It's not about being able to pay the fine. I just didn't want to be the reason you got in trouble."

Too late, sweetheart, I'm already in trouble—can't get you off my friggin' mind.

He stilled her hand on his thigh by covering it with his. He lifted it to his lips and kissed her knuckles before releasing her. Touching her too much would land him in more trouble than he needed. Touching her would drop him to his knees.

Daren pulled up outside Club Perform and passed the keys and sizeable tip to the valet before opening the door for Cassandra and taking her hand. He led her to the front door where the security staff welcomed him with the handshakes and chest butts men used in lieu of hugs. He kept Cassandra close to him while gauging just how comfortable she was. If she wanted to leave then they would instantly. But her eyes were filled with excitement as she looked around while a bouncer wrapped a black plastic wristband around her hand before they were allowed entry. Once inside the club they headed to the bar. Daren knew all the employees here, and Club Perform catered to a more elite clientele. There'd be no scumbags pawing at Cassandra. Everyone here was screened before entry.

Normally, Daren would've taken Cassandra out dancing to one of her favorite nightspots on the other side of town. The kind of club that was just for dancing and drinking and would never allow the sexual atmosphere Club Perform offered. But he'd been compelled to share a glimpse of his lifestyle with her, and Club Perform would be the most desirable place to start. While it accommodated the BDSM scene, it wasn't as hardcore as most fetish clubs. She needed a place to feel comfortable and allow herself to have fun because, unless he was way off his mark, he sensed she hid her own desires and fantasies. And he doubted there was anthing vanilla about them.

At Club Perform, couples could engage in an array of sexual trysts to fulfill their fantasies or fetishes. It wouldn't be uncommon, once the night grew later, to find people fucking up against the walls, at the tables, or even on the dance floor. Many lucky Doms would receive blowjobs from their subs as they sat at their table, the sub on her knees sucking his cock at his command. He couldn't wait to see the expression on Cassandra's face when she played voyeur to such sexual acts for the first time.

Then there were the private rooms in the back that guests could rent by the hour or for the entire night. Liquor service ended at 2:00 a.m., but by then the crowd was fueled on enough alcohol and hormones to last them until closing time. Maybe Daren would consider renting one of those rooms for an hour and give Cassandra her birthday spanking after all. Now there was a thought to ponder. His dick came to life again.

Smiling, he handed Cassandra her drink and led them to a table by the dance floor. The fast pulse of the music emanated from a dozen speakers and the songs were chosen to entice customers to swing rhythmically on the dance floor. He couldn't wait to get her out there. They'd danced plenty of times, so he knew she had sweet moves. His cock flexed in agreement.

"This isn't so bad, Daren," Cassandra said, then sipped her drink. "You've always made your love life sound so dark and forbidden."

He offered half a smile. Dark and forbidden. If she only knew how good that could be. "This isn't my love life, babe. This is just a club I frequent to relax and meet people."

Watching as she sucked on the straw made him wish he was the thin plastic drink stirrer.

"Meet women you mean."

"Ah, be careful, Cass, or you'll sound like the jealous one."

She smiled, a sarcastic grin meant to intimidate. "Hardly. Besides, there's nothing these women have that I don't."

While he watched her nervously twirl her straw, he spoke. "True. But these women like things, well sex, a little rougher, a little dirtier, and much darker."

"Maybe I do, too."

Breathe he reminded himself. "Not like this, Cass."

She frowned. "How would you know what I like? You've never asked."

His cock hardened like steel. "Believe me, Cass, I'd know if you were into the Dominant/submissive lifestyle."

She surveyed the room. "Well, I'll admit, I've never considered it before, but now you've raised my curiosity. I like to try new things and life has been a bit boring lately. Maybe this is just what I need."

He swallowed so hard that he checked to see if his tongue was still there. Did he just hear her right?

"Come on, bad boy. Dance with me," Cassandra demanded, taking his hand and leading the way onto the dance floor.

Okay, on the dance floor they were an even match. This he could handle. Or so he thought. Once she started gyrating her hips and moving her body to the beat of the music, he was a lost man. Lost in the vision of her body swaying in that sexy red dress. Lost in the smile plastered on her face as she swung in a circle, her hair flying around her. Lost totally and completely in her pleasure.

His hands gripped her waist and pulled her hard against him as the music changed to a low drumbeat. He held her pelvis to his cock, allowing her to ride him as her hips bucked against him. Those hard nipples plastered against her dress glided over his chest with her every move, adding to his sweet torture. Her smile faded, replaced by a knowing grin like that of a woman who had a man under her spell. Well, two could play that game.

His hands glided over her hips up to her ribs, up further to skim his thumbs along the side of her breasts, appreciating the gentle swell of her perfect tits. He was pleased with the way her eyes widened in acknowledgment, the way heat flared within the brown depths. Was she wet?

Quickly, he spun her around, holding her back to his chest as one arm wrapped tightly around her waist and the other on her shoulder. Her ass rocked back into his cock, sending a river of fire through his body, stealing his breath. His fingers splayed low over her flat belly, the soft material of her dress silky to touch. Her hand stroked the back of his neck as her fingernails gently scraped his skin, driving his arousal higher.

He hoped she felt the length of him as he ground into her ass. His hands moved up and down her thighs, over the dress to bare skin. She was smooth as the finest silk, hot as the brightest flame. His face found the curve of her neck and nuzzled her. She smelled delicious—lilacs and vanilla would never be the same for him. He heard nothing but his heartbeat, felt nothing but the awesome sensation of her slender body molded to his.

When she shimmied down his body and back up again, it was all he could do not to find a wall to fuck her against. God, his cock had never been so hard or so desperate. He reminded himself that this was his best friend and not some woman who understood the darker kind of sex he'd be expecting. But it was like he actually just met Cassandra because she was showing him a side he'd never seen before. This side of her was sensual, sexy, and downright desirable.

He twirled her to face him, seizing her arms behind her back as he held her to his chest. Her eyes flashed with a bolt of lust and her head swung back displaying the alluring side of her long neck. His teeth wanted to sink into that sensitive skin. She was at his mercy with her hands immovable, but he regained control of his desires and released her.

She was his best friend. Maybe if he kept chanting that in his head, his cock would back off of its pursuit of her.

Taking her by the hand, he led her back to their table.

She picked up her drink and pointed a finger. "You know, I wasn't done dancing, Daren. Next time you might want to ask me if I want to be dragged off the dance floor."

Jesus Christ, she was inciting the Dominant in him so fiercely that she was lucky he didn't blister her ass right here. Talk like that would earn her a damn good paddling if she were his sub. He was used to calling the shots, not getting lectured by the woman he was with.

Damn, he would love to tone that attitude of hers down. He smiled at the thought. She'd give him the challenge of a fucking lifetime. He wasn't a fool not to realize what it would take to tame a woman like Cassandra, her backbone being just one of many obstacles. And that mouth. That beautiful mouth could open at any time and tear him a new asshole. God, he'd welcome that challenge. She was exactly what he'd been looking for in these damn clubs for all those lonely nights, the ideal woman who eluded him.

Why did the woman of his most erotic dreams have to be right under his nose the whole time? And why did it have to be the one woman he couldn't have? Fuck!

"I needed a drink," he said plainly before discreetly adjusting his cock.

"So? Do I have to hold your hand while you get it?" Her eyes spit fire. He loved it. "I said I wanted to dance tonight, and that's what I'm going to do."

Cassandra strutted back onto the dance floor as the multitude of strobe lights glided over her skin, illuminating it. As she danced with the crowd, her slender body moved effortlessly to the rhythm. Daren was completely mesmerized by her. But she wasn't at one of her typical nightspots where sex waited until the couple got home. She was out of her element here and, just as he expected, it took under a minute before another man approached her.

Make that two men.

He should rescue her, but he wanted to see what she would do. And he didn't have to worry. There were rules here. So he watched carefully, never taking his eyes off of her. The two men sandwiched her, front and back, inching closer with each beat of the music. Cassandra cast Daren a wary look before turning back to her partners and shimmying between them.

Aw hell. She didn't have to enjoy it so damn much.

While he couldn't hear her laughter over the music, he could see that she was having a blast. Cassandra was the star of the room, every guy noticing her presence. Strangely though, Daren wasn't worried because everyone understood the rules. And the number one rule was clearly dangling from Cassandra's wrist. That simple plastic band clearly marked her as taken. She was Daren's for the night.

When Daren calmly walked onto the dance floor and claimed her waist, the other two men melted back into the gyrating crowd.

He enjoyed the look of surprise on her face. "Were you expecting them to arm wrestle me for you?"

She shrugged, wrapping her arms around his neck. "Kind of, I guess."

"Don't worry, baby. Under normal circumstances, I'm sure they would've wanted to do me bodily harm for stealing you away."

"Under normal circumstances?"

"Different kind of club, Cass. Different set of rules."

"And what would those rules be?"

He held her hand out. "This bracelet signals to every male, and female, that you're taken."

Her mouth opened wide. "Taken? What the hell do you mean taken?"

He laughed because he should've expected this reaction. She'd never accept being claimed by anyone. Even by him.

His hips swayed into hers as the beat of the music

increased. "A club like this must have firm rules. It keeps everyone safe. Keeps things orderly."

She shrugged free of him and walked back to the table, her hips revealing her temper as they swayed back and forth, each step she took was more determined than the last. He followed closely.

"You still didn't answer my question," she demanded, her voice loud enough to be heard over the music.

He watched her for a moment, seeing the anger in her eyes flare. "That bracelet serves as a symbol. You arrived with me, so by wearing it, all the other patrons know you're with somebody and not to hit on you."

"I'm *with* someone. I'm not *taken!*" she said between clenched teeth.

"You're right. Do you want to leave?"

She shook her head. "No. I want this bracelet off. I'm not taken. What if the love of my life is here in this crowd? Wearing this stupid thing would prevent him from hitting on me."

Now jealousy rose like bile in his throat. "And you don't think me being by your side would prevent him from hitting on you?"

Her chin rose three inches, clearly defiant. And totally turning him on. "Different kind of club. Different set of rules," she repeated his words. "You said so yourself, Daren. If I'm not wearing this stupid bracelet then everyone here will know I'm not taken."

"Enough!" His tone obviously caught her off-guard as she clamped her lips tightly. "You'll wear that damn bracelet or we'll leave. You don't know this scene like I do, Cass, so you'll listen or we leave. Understood?"

Now, why he thought talking sternly to her would make her listen was beyond him. But when that sweet smile creased her lips, he knew he wasn't going to like her response.

"I understand, Daren."

She what? Every brain cell warned him to tread lightly. But the Dominant in him took pride in having Cassandra comply with his wishes.

Taking her hand, he caressed her knuckles as they leaned over the table. "Thank you, Cass. I know you don't understand this, but it's for the best."

She smiled sweetly again. "You have a good night, Daren. I'm going home." She abruptly yanked her hand from his.

Damn it! He should have suspected something when she gave in so damn easily.

"Cass? We don't have to leave."

"I don't give a shit what you do. I'm leaving."

She elbowed her way through the crowd to the door. Daren stayed right on her heel. Stomping through the door, she stepped onto the sidewalk and asked the valet for a taxi.

"Lady's all set. I'll just take my car," Daren said, handing his ticket and another sizeable tip to the valet who disappeared quickly.

Tapping her foot, arms crossed, she stared at him dangerously. "So now this stupid bracelet means you can tell me how I can get home?"

His patience was wearing thin. "We'll talk about this in the car."

"The hell we will. I don't want to talk to you. Some birthday."

Cassandra grasped the band and stretched the

plastic until she could pull it over her hand. Then she threw it at Daren. His hand automatically caught it and shoved it in his pants pocket. His eyes watched her, his cock throbbing at her defiance. God, had he ever been so turned on?

The valet pulled up with his car and Daren opened the door for Cassandra. She took her seat without even a glance at him. As soon as he was behind the wheel, he peeled away from the curb and merged into traffic.

"I'm sorry, Cass."

His apology was met with silence. That was never a good sign. She loved to talk. More than that, she loved to argue. Now, she wouldn't even look at him. He'd screwed this night up royally. Trying to show her a glimpse of his lifestyle was such a bad idea in hindsight.

"So what are you sorry for?" she finally asked after a few minutes.

He dared to look at her and was relieved that she was no longer staring out the side window, but at least looking through the windshield. He'd take whatever progress he could if it meant she'd forgive him.

"I'm sorry for ruining your birthday. I shouldn't have taken you there. We should've gone to one of your regular spots."

"Did I say I was upset you took me there? No. I didn't. I'm pissed because you marked me as taken—something I'm clearly not—by a man who would only rub against me on the dance floor."

His hand gripped the steering wheel. "As your best friend, it wouldn't be appropriate to do anything more to you."

"Oh, please. With your lifestyle, you're worried

about what's appropriate?"

"You're damn right I am when it involves you." He took a long, steadying breath. "Christ, I know I've totally screwed up tonight, but do you think you can leave a shred of my manhood in place and not make me beg. Right now I feel lower than scum."

She fell silent again.

"Cass."

She sighed softly, a sure sign her temper was deflating. "You're not scum, Daren. I forgive you. I even understand your motives. You just wanted me to have fun and be safe doing so. You're the best friend a girl could have. But I am an adult. Remember that." She patted his hand. "You can make it up to me by taking me for pizza and then coming back to my place for a glass of wine."

Relief flooded him. "That, baby, sounds like the best idea tonight." He drove to the closest pizza place, planning to eat fast. He didn't need any more public spectacles tonight.

Chapter Two

Unlocking her front door, Cassandra turned off the alarm before heading into the kitchen. She poured two glasses of wine and walked into the living room handing Daren his as he sat on the couch. She joined him after kicking off her heels. Her feet were grateful to be free. Curling her legs under her, she faced him and sipped her wine.

He looked so tense that she wanted to massage the stress from his muscles. Her palms tingled at the thought of running over that hard body.

She tried to speak normally but was afraid her voice was breathless from sitting this close to him. "That pizza hit the spot. I was starving. Now, I think we need music. I still have the beat from the club pumping through me," she quipped, setting her wine glass down before standing and moving over to the stereo. "Any requests?"

"Just that you get that pretty little ass back over here. I owe you a birthday spanking. Or did you think I forgot?"

She smiled back and adjusted the volume so the song wouldn't drown out their conversation. "You wouldn't dare."

He stood after placing his wine glass next to hers

and advanced on her, the look on his face both playful and menacing.

She yelped and ran in the opposite direction, but he quickly followed.

"Oh, I dare, Cass. You've been testing my patience all night."

She circled the coffee table. "Really? Too bad. Besides, I thought you said it was a birthday spanking."

The grin he flashed was devious. "It is. Or it started out as one. Now, I just want to spank you."

Standing with only the slim table between them, Cass didn't feel the confidence she boasted.

"You're going to cream your panties, baby, when I put you across my lap and paddle your bottom."

She giggled, the vision his words conjured had her backside tingling, begging for his words to be true. Looking at him now, she didn't doubt that he meant it. But in case he just meant to tease, then she'd give it right back.

Still hovering over the table, she spoke with a hint of breathlessness. "Now that would be an ideal birthday gift. Definitely one to remember."

He grinned wide, his eyes sparkling with mischief. "Then your wish is my command, sweetheart."

Her heart pounded with expectation. "Oh? Will this spanking be on my bare bottom?"

She was pleased when he inhaled sharply.

His brown eyes sharpened as his lips quirked at the corner. "Would love that, but since this is your first spanking, I'll allow it over your dress. Since you've just turned twenty-nine, I'd say that firm ass of yours is gonna be red hot and glowing by the time I get done.

Oh, and, of course, one extra *hard* spank for good luck."

"Of course," she agreed eagerly. "But that's only if you can catch me."

She shrieked when he growled and lunged. She ran one way, then the other, managing to avoid his groping hands. But her luck ran out when he simply leaned over the table and locked a powerful arm around her waist and lifted her over the obstacle. His other arm swung under her knees and he cradled her to his chest while her hands clung to his shoulders.

She was giggling so hard, she hardly noticed that he'd walked to the couch. When he placed her on her feet and sat on the couch, she swallowed hard.

Oh, man. This was really going to happen.

Without a word, he hauled her over his lap before she could let out a protest. She gasped in shock, her long, brown hair hanging to the floor and shielding her face. Part of her fantasy was really coming true! Breathe. Just breathe. For Christ's sake, don't pass out and ruin the moment, she demanded of herself. But hanging off his legs made her feel silly.

Her hand clung to his pants near his lower leg. "Daren, stop this and let me up."

"Cass," Daren's low voice hovered near her ear. "I want you to enjoy this. I need you to trust me, baby. Okay?"

"Y-yes," she said, wondering if she could actually go through with this when her pussy was already convulsing sharply. If she could only come right now, then she could enjoy the spanking instead of being strung as taut as a yo-yo. As it was, her body was on fire, and everywhere Daren touched was pure pleasurable torture. Even the way his hand held her on his lap was arousing.

"Cass?"

"Ummm."

"Baby, I'm gonna enjoy spanking you. It'll feel a bit uncomfortable at first but, if you trust me, it'll be very pleasurable. Trust me to do this right. But if you really and truly want me to stop, just say stop. I promise that I will instantly."

It took her a moment to realize his hand was resting on her ass as he talked. She was now draped across her best friend's lap—the man she'd lusted after for too long to remember—with her ass right under his nose.

She squirmed automatically. "Daren, maybe this isn't a good idea. I don't want my dress ruined."

"I'll buy you another one."

"That's not the point. The point is…ow!" He was really spanking her. Oh. My. God!

"That's one," he announced smugly.

"Daren!"

Without warning, his large hand landed on her right cheek. The pain was noticeable, but not unbearable. Her pussy reacted immediately, tightening and throbbing. Another spank landed on her left cheek. His hand rubbed over her dress before landing two much harder slaps. After each set of spanks, Daren caressed her bottom and the intimate gesture shot fire through her belly to her cunt where her juices already coated her pussy lips. Her vaginal walls quivered with every stroke he landed on her ass and the intense need to come robbed the breath from her lungs.

"Happy Birthday, baby. Hope all your wishes

come true."

God, if he'd just stick that hard cock pressing against her thigh into her throbbing pussy, one of those dreams would come true. Before she could finish her thoughts, his hand picked up the pace and the caresses became fewer. The burn was better than she'd imagined. The even tempo made the wet folds of her pussy convulse, keeping rhythm with his hand. He showed no mercy with his evenly paced spanks, alternating globes. She loved every second.

Cassandra bit her lip to keep from crying out in pleasure, fearing he would think he was hurting her and stop his delicious attentions.

Cool air floated over her hot bottom. Oh shit! Her dress had ridden up from her wiggling. His palm connected with bare skin on the lower part of her cheek. The sensation was so much better than it had been over the material of the dress.

She moaned, the simple sound so erotic she couldn't believe it had come from her.

"Oh my God, Cass! You're…wet," Daren said, his voice raw and deep. "You're panties are soaked, baby."

Her body ceased the playful wiggling instantly. Heat flooded her face and embarrassment consumed her. Daren had seen her panties? Her very wet panties? How could she ever face him again? She had to get up.

When she attempted to climb off his lap, his strong arm held her in place. "You're not going anywhere, Cass. I'm not finished." His hand slowly caressed her butt cheek, the intimate touch building her arousal to an intensity that threatened to destroy her.

"Daren!"

"You know the rule, Cass. If you want me to stop, you need to say so. Squirming only excites me more."

His hand landed sharply on her bottom only to be followed by more. The orgasm snuck up without warning and bright lights exploded behind her closed eyes. Her body trembled violently, and her scream penetrated the otherwise quiet room. The only other sound was the steady spanks to her burning ass and the soft beat of the music. The warm, slow descent of pussy juices leaked onto the thin strip of panties and the smaller orgasms clenched her cunt until she ached.

When her panties slid over her hot bottom, the scratch of the material left the sensitive skin tingling more.

"What the hell are you doing, Daren?"

She felt his hand soothing the bare, hot skin of her butt cheeks and bit her bottom lip again to keep from crying out at the delightful pleasure.

"I couldn't resist taking a peek at my work. Your creamy skin is now a dark pink and marked with my handprints. I wish you could see it. This is the most erotic sight ever."

"Hard to see hanging upside down. Let me up." Did that husky voice belong to her?

"You've got to learn, baby, that I give the orders and you take them."

"Like hell. I didn't sign on as your sub, Daren."

"But you would be an amazing one, baby. All that temper and attitude. Mmmmm. The pleasure I'd have taming you."

She punched at his lower legs. "Damn it! I said let me up." She stilled. "Wh-what are you doing?"

His laugh teased her oversensitive nerves. "I don't

think you really need me to answer that, but what the hell? It'll be erotic to explain to you how I'm touching you."

Cassandra moaned as Daren slid a long finger along the slick folds of her pussy, tormenting her with a need she could only describe as feral.

"Feel my fingertip circle your clit. Feel me smooth your juices over it."

"Mmmmm."

"Do you like it when I squeeze and pinch the tender bud?"

To her utter disbelief and shock, she cried out as she exploded again with an orgasm as strong and powerful as its predecessor. She never wanted this feeling to end. The man she loved was pleasuring her and now she wanted—no needed—to be fucked hard by him.

"I'll take that as a yes," he said and laughed. "Six more spanks left, Cass. You gonna be able to handle them?" Daren asked, not removing his finger from her cunt, but inserting it deeper to the first knuckle. Never had a man's touch been so intimate, never had it meant so much.

"God, don't stop now, Daren. Please. I need you." She didn't care if she begged. Hell, she'd fucking plead with him on her knees as long as he didn't stop.

He laughed softly, his breath tickling her ear as he leaned down to whisper. "I need you too, Cass. Maybe if you're a good girl, I'll spread these creamy thighs of yours and bury my hard cock deep inside you after your spanking. Think you can handle me, baby?"

She understood his question. The evidence of his arousal was jammed into the side of her belly as she lay helplessly over his lap.

"I'll take you just fine." Her voice was so breathless that she barely recognized her words.

By the way his cock flexed against her, she figured he heard them clearly. The last six spanks were administered in rapid fashion with no caresses, and the burn of her punished bottom was exhilarating and soaked her pussy all over again.

He was breathing hard. His muscles rigid and tense under her.

For a long moment, Daren gently rubbed her stinging backside before surprising her with a solid, hard spank in the middle of her ass, causing a scream to escape her lips.

"That was for good luck," Daren announced, his deep voice humming with tension.

Blind with lust, she couldn't even remember her damn name. She could feel him making her decent again, tenderly pulling her panties into place and straightening her dress before setting her into standing position.

Daren stood in front of Cassandra with his hands on his hips and wearing a shit-eating grin. "You're one fucking hot woman, Cass."

She couldn't look at him. Embarrassment filled her. He'd seen her wet panties and bare ass. He'd spanked her, caressing and soothing her bottom. The delicious feeling still thrilled her. Christ, he'd had his fingers inside her and now it looked like that was all she'd get. Why wasn't he ripping of her damn clothes? Reality was quickly becoming too much to handle as it mixed with her fantasies.

Cassandra faced Daren, her chin out. "Really?

And you're just now noticing?" she demanded and stormed past him to walk into the kitchen with the wine glasses. Her sore bottom reminded her of his treatment with every step, heating her pussy all over again.

His heavy footsteps behind her warned that he was quickly following. "Hell no. I've noticed for a long time that my best friend has the nicest ass I've ever seen on a woman, one that was definitely made for spanking."

She whirled around quickly to face him, her temper building. "Oh, really?"

"Yeah. Really." Daren crossed his arms over his chest, his expression as serious as she'd ever seen it. "I've also noticed that my best friend has a hot body, her breasts would fit perfectly in my hands, her neck was made for slow sucking, and her legs would wrap nicely around my waist."

"What?" Her voice cracked.

His gaze studied her intensely for a long moment before he spoke again. "I've wanted you in my bed forever, Cass." He stepped closer to hold her in front of him, his breathing labored. "If you don't feel the same way, I'll understand and put an end to the rest of my plans for tonight, including fucking you until neither of us can walk."

She stared with wide eyes, his admission stealing her thoughts of anything but him. "I want you, too, Daren. Please don't tease me."

Before she knew what he intended, his head dipped the few inches for his lips to touch hers. The hard, searing kiss buckled her knees, but his free arm wrapped quickly around her waist, holding her against his toned body. His tongue traced along the line of her mouth, demanding that she open.

It took her only a few seconds to realize this was happening, not a dream. Her mouth obliged, giving him instant access. He took immediate control again, forcing her back against the counter, tongue fucking her mouth with rapid, firm movements. The scent of her roses meshed with his musky cologne.

She attempted to breathe, but only managed to suck in gasps of air as Daren deepened the kiss, his tongue stroking hers, whipping around like a loose electrical wire. Everywhere it touched, every stroke it pleasured her with, sent sizzling shock waves deep into her belly and her cunt lips clenching in anticipation of fulfillment.

He tasted of wine and heat, the flavors intoxicating her. Daren was a man ready to fuck a woman. Cassandra just happened to be the woman in his arms. Finally! She returned his kiss with a ferocity of her own, every desire she'd ever hidden from him finally breaking free. She took immense satisfaction when he moaned, the sound vibrating from his throat.

As suddenly as he began the kiss, he ended it but kept her in place and only moved back far enough to gaze into her eyes.

Breathing heavily, she sucked in deep bursts of air, but the oxygen didn't make it to her brain. She felt light headed and gloriously giddy. Very, very aroused, Cassandra lunged. Wrapping her arms around his neck, she kissed him with all the passion she'd bottled up over the years.

She was weightless, like she was floating on air, and quickly realized Daren was carrying her. He broke the kiss long enough to walk into the living room, which was closer than her bedroom. The apartment illuminated only by the lights in the kitchen and living room, the darkness of the night masked her fears as her fantasy to became reality. She needed to fuck Daren. She didn't need to think now.

With little regard for chivalry, Daren released Cassandra roughly onto the couch and towered over her.

His hand fisted in the front of her dress. With a quick tug of his wrist, he lifted the dress over her head. Cool air hit the exposed skin of her chest. One strong hand palmed her breast through her lace bra before expertly reaching behind and unsnapping the hook. Her breasts burst free as the bra floated to the floor. His mouth was locked to hers, their tongues wrestling in a heated match. Her world spun on its axis as reality mixed with fantasy.

Daren's fingers pinched and tugged her nipple hard enough that she moaned into his kiss. With hands moving in a blur of activity, she quickly tugged at his clothes, pulling them free of his body until he was gloriously naked.

His hands skimmed down her back over the heated flesh of her bottom, rubbing and soothing while inching the panties over her hips. When the thin silk material reached her knees, she shook her legs free of them.

Naked, they collapsed onto the couch, his body over hers, sinking deeply into the plush, dark blue cushions.

"Now, Daren. Fuck me now. I want your cock in me. Oh God, I've always wanted you. Deep. Hard.

Fast."

Daren moaned and picked up his discarded pants. "I wanted our first time together to be more than a quickie, baby. I just don't think I'll last longer than a few strokes. You're so fucking hot."

He quickly unwrapped a condom and sheathed his anxious cock before placing it against the bare entrance of her pussy. When his stare caught hers, she could see the question in his eyes. Did they want to really do this? Did they want to cross a line that meant they couldn't go back?

Oh God, yes!

She raised her hips in silent pleading. With a slight grin, he plunged into her slick, pulsing pussy. Arching to take the length of him, Cassandra screamed in pleasure, her fingernails biting into the hard flesh of his shoulders. Sweat slicked their joined bodies as his muscular thighs rapidly pumped his thick rod into her drenched cunt, every stroke deeper, harder, fueled by pent-up lust.

Cassandra writhed under the weight of Daren's body, her pussy contracting instinctually in response to his cock's glorious invasion. Her body stretched to accommodate his thickness. She could feel his heat through the latex condom. Every thrust of his cock into her channel caressed nerve endings along her vaginal walls, the pleasure new and thrilling. Never had she accomplished this burning desire with her vibrator.

She flexed her fingers through his thick, wavy hair. The dark brown locks offered a means to pull his lips to hers. He accepted her invitation with fervor. Crushing his lips to hers, he moaned. Opening, she gave full access for his tongue to claim her mouth. His tongue raked over her teeth, cheeks, and tongue, searching every inch and tasting all of her.

Her lungs begged for air, but she refused to break the connection. His kisses infused more life into her than breathing ever could. With exquisite manipulation of her mouth, he showed her what it was like to breathe fire. He taught her where every erotic zone was hidden in her mouth, claiming her with his passion.

Breaking the kiss, Daren trailed his lips down Cassandra's throat while she gasped for air. She slowly released her hold on his hair as he descended her body to rest his lips over her breast. With his cock purposely stroking long and hard into her pussy, he used his mouth to add to her delicious torment. His tongue stiffened to lick her erect nipple, as a silent signal raced to her clit and began a slow hum. Oh God, could a woman actually die from the need to orgasm? Cassandra was beginning to think so.

Daren licked and laved each nipple, alternating back and forth. Using devastatingly long circles, his tongue washed over each areola and the sensation strummed through her belly to her womb. If only she could always keep his mouth on her skin. His strong fingers lifted each breast to his mouth, squeezing and kneading. Her hand burrowed into his thick hair to hold him close.

The narrow couch should have restricted their movements, but it only kept their bodies entwined. She loved the feel of his entire weight on her. He was solid, hard, tense. Every muscle her hands roamed over was taut and rigid. She closed her eyes and let her fingers map out the rough angles of his body, committing them to memory. His body shifted again, muscles flexing under her palms, his skin hot to the touch. His face burrowed into the side of her neck and his warm breath sent delightful chills down her back. She inhaled deeply, enjoying his musky cologne mixing with the scent of sex.

She clung to his upper body, her hands around his shoulders and back. She appreciated how well he maneuvered his cock to tease places hidden deep inside her pussy that she didn't even know existed. God, she wanted to come! Needed to come! If she didn't, she would surely detonate into a million pieces from the pleasure rioting through her body.

"Oh Christ, Cass. You feel too fucking good. Fuck."

His hands gripped her waist as he rode into her, his pace quickening, but even and deliberate. One hand moved swiftly between their bodies. His finger flicked over her clit, the unexpected touch causing a cry to escape from her throat. Her mind reeled from the sharp jolt her clit sent through her body and then protested when he removed his hand.

Her orgasm was building fast now. All the energies in her body banded together, forming a bond that would destroy her when it erupted. Her breasts tingled from his sucking, her lips swelled from his kisses, her heart pounded, and her blood raged through her veins like hot lava. Every part of her body was aware of Daren's cock buried to the hilt inside her, driving her orgasm up the Richter scale.

"Daren! Daren! Daren!"

Her body was possessed, that's the only excuse for not recognizing the feelings riveting through her. Wonderful, glorious feelings. All she could see was the top of his head and his firm ass moving up and down as his hips slammed into hers.

"Come for me, Cass. Come for me, baby."

She wanted to. It was right on the edge, but not within reach.

"Noooo. Oh, Daren…please…oh, Daren!"

When his finger found her clit again and added pressure, she exploded. Just like that, she was taken on a wild ride. He stiffened and jerked his hips hard into her softness and held his length deep inside. Her cunt responded violently. Deep within her womb a fuse lit, the charge flared to life and burst forward with an orgasm so powerful she trembled and shook like a rag doll in an earthquake. Barely finished with her release, Daren's solid, damp body collapsed onto her, his breathing heavy and his cock softening until it slid from her pussy's grip.

When they finally gained strength, they pulled away from each other. What had she just done? What had *they* just done?

She dared to look at Daren as he discarded the condom into the wrapper before sitting back against her couch, his head lying against the tall cushion and his chest rising sharply with his breaths. His eyes were closed, his skin covered in a light sheen of perspiration. He looked absolutely mouth watering.

She just fucked her best friend! The man who for years had haunted her dreams nightly. The man who spanked her! Christ, her ass still tingled from where his hand left its mark.

What should she do now? Let him fall asleep naked on her couch? Sneak off to her room and quietly pray he doesn't regret tonight?

Before she could do anything, his eyes opened sleepily as his arm reached for her. "I know what you're thinking, so stop it." He pulled her humming body against his side, cuddling her firmly.

"You do? Then what am I thinking?"

He chuckled, his hand moving slowly up and down her arm, while he shut his eyes again. "You're thinking of running and hiding from me. That we can forget tonight ever happened."

She opened her mouth in shock, but no words came out.

His head turned and his eyes opened halfway. "Told you I knew what was going on in that pretty little head. I'm telling you, I have no regrets and neither will you."

"Don't tell me what to feel, Daren."

"Wouldn't dream of it, baby. But I will tell you that you won't regret tonight. You won't regret fucking me and I won't regret fucking you. Because it's something we've both wanted for a long time and finally had the balls to act on it."

He pulled her head close and kissed her forehead.

"Daren?"

"Hmmm."

"This was the best birthday ever."

He laughed, stood, and lifted her into his arms. He carried her to her bedroom and gently placed her on the bed. She scooted her bottom up as he pulled the covers down then placed them over her and joined her.

"Tell me your wildest fantasies, Cass," Daren said, lying sideways watching her.

She turned her head to stare at him and basked in the knowledge that she'd just fucked this man she'd known forever. And he could fuck so good.

When she didn't answer, Daren frowned and spoke again. "Cass, I'm not going to let you regret making love with me. I've wanted you forever. What just happened was so hot, baby, just thinking of it has my cock growing hard for you again."

Making love? They only fucked. There was a difference. "I agree, tonight was, well, very nice. Better than my dreams."

He smiled, his eyes lighting up. "Do tell."

She laughed, shaking her head. "I'm not telling you anything."

He grasped a strand of her hair and twirled it. "I'll tell you what I want to do to you."

"You've given that thought, have you?"

He frowned. "Hell yeah. More times than I can remember."

"Do tell."

He smiled again. "After you. I did ask first. Start with your fantasies. I want to know what Cassandra desires. I want to know all your secrets."

His voice lulled her into such a state of relaxation that she was surprised she wasn't sleeping. But truth be told, she was full of energy and filled with a zest for life.

"Come on, Cass. Tell me your fantasies. I'm not known for my patience. You're going to have to learn that."

"And you'll have to learn that I could care less."

He laughed, a deep, hearty sound. "God, you are amazing. You give new meaning to a woman with balls."

She turned completely on her side to face him.

"Do you really want to know, Daren? You won't laugh at me?"

His face became serious. "I would never laugh at you for sharing your intimate self with me, Cassandra. Don't ever think like that again."

Her hand toyed with his curly chest hairs. "Sorry, it's just that, well, tonight has been a whirlwind of emotions. I mean I just fucked my best friend. You spanked me, for crying out loud."

His laugh was contagious. "You liked that, didn't you? I know you did. If not, you wouldn't have come while laying across my lap."

"Oh God. Yes, I liked it."

He smiled wickedly, his gaze roaming her face. "Good. Because I enjoyed paddling that pretty little ass. There's more of that to come. I happen to like the feel of your soft flesh quivering under my palm as I smack down on those beautiful cheeks."

More to come? That caught her interest. "I gathered that much."

"It was a bonus when your dress rode up. I almost came in my pants at the sight of those sexy panties damp with your juices."

"I wanted to crawl into a corner."

He laughed and tweaked her nose. "Now tell me *all* your fantasies."

Her cheeks flamed and her eyes avoided his. "I have wondered what it would be like to be tied up." She suddenly wanted to share all her secrets with him, hoping he'd stay for more than one night of fun. "You've already spanked me so you fulfilled one already."

"So you do have a submissive side to you, huh?

Interesting."

"Why do you say that? Just because I want to be held down and fucked like I was the most beautiful woman in the world?"

The tiny creases near his eyes blended an edginess to his handsome looks. "Yes. If you didn't want to be submissive, then you'd just want to be fucked and not held down to do it. You want to give up control, Cass. That's all it means. You want your lover to pleasure you without interference or resistance from you."

"Well, when you say it like that, it doesn't sound so bad."

"Calling you a submissive, or a sub, isn't meant as an insult. A submissive lover is the most sensual lover a Dominant master can hope for. It's what I've spent my life looking for without much luck."

Did she hear him right? "What do you mean you haven't found a woman? You go through women like socks. One a day, maybe a pair a day."

His face was so serious, almost pained. "Maybe they go through me, Cass. Ever consider that? Maybe they get what they can out of me in bed before they fully realize my dark sexual desires and lose interest. Then they hightail it out of there."

Wasn't that what she planned to do? Run as soon as their fun was over before getting her heart broken? "Yeah right! Have you looked in the mirror lately? You're quite a catch, Daren."

Lifting her hand to his mouth, he kissed her knuckles. "I wonder where this new side of you will lead if you allowed yourself to embrace your sexuality. It's okay to have fantasies. It's okay to want more than just vanilla sex."

She swallowed hard, not believing her openness. "I know. I haven't complained about my sex life, Daren. I've had orgasms before. I've had great sex before."

"But?"

A long sigh didn't help her feel any better. "It just never seemed satisfying. Like there's this yearning deep inside me, like a damn itch you can't reach."

"I understand completely. Any other desires or wishes?"

She shrugged. "That's about it. Well, maybe trying anal sex. Never did that, but I think I'd like to. Heard it's painful, though."

He stared. "I'll make sure that request moves to the top of the priority list." He ran a finger over her cheek. "With the right preparation, you'd enjoy the hell out of a good ass-fucking. I'd love to fuck that tight virgin hole. The thought of it has me hard as a hammer. I'm not kidding, baby. Reach down and feel. I could drill nails with it."

Her hand slid beneath the covers to caress his erection. "You weren't lying."

He yanked her on top of his chest. Fisting his hand in her hair, he pulled her mouth to his for a hard kiss on her lips. The sheer strength of him flowed through his kiss. The way his tongue always manipulated hers, displaying its power, while taking the breath from her.

But she was feeling a little wanton. She placed her hands on both sides of his face, the hint of beard breaking through his skin and tickling her hands. Holding him still, she slowly moved her lips over his, gently nipping his lower lip then licking it with her tongue. Running her tongue along his teeth, she probed

51

deeper into his mouth, thrilled when his breath sucked in hard. His hands slipped down her body to grip her sides, his fingers kneading, grasping.

Her tongue slowly danced in his mouth, up and down, side to side, top to bottom. The hot taste of his mouth only encouraged her to continue her slow torment. Feeling his cock flex under her belly, signaled she'd done her job.

She pulled back, breathing heavy.

He pulled away, breathless. "Damn, baby. I'm gonna love this friends-with-benefits deal."

Her heart ached. Her throat constricted. "Is that what we have?"

"Damn right. We have our friendship and the best sex ever." His hand cupped her ass and squeezed. The intimate gesture fell short of meaning what it would've only a minute ago.

He hadn't made any romantic declarations to her other than admitting his physical attraction. So she had no right to be mad at his honest admission. He was right. They were friends. They were having sex. That was a benefit. Then why the hell did she crave so much more from him? Why did she want him all to herself? Why did she want forever instead of a few days?

Putting her best poker face on, she smiled and played out her part of the equation. She'd take her fill of him until he decided to leave her bed like he'd done to every other woman. But damn it if she didn't want to fuck him 24/7 until she got him out of her system.

She couldn't help herself, she had to touch him again. "I want to taste your cock in my mouth. Now," she demanded, moving down his body, straddling his lower legs, and removing the sheet to reveal an erect, thick cock. Her small hand held the fat head, stroking slowly over the purplish veins.

His body stiffened. "Yes, baby."

She heard a package ripping. "What are you doing?"

His hands stilled and his eyes caught hers. "Don't you want me to put a condom on?"

She stared, her hand holding his cock tenderly. "Do I need you to?"

He lifted his head to look down his body to meet her eyes. "Not at all. I've never gone bareback with anyone, not even for blowjobs. I'm clean. If I didn't think so, I wouldn't give you an option on the condom."

Smiling, her hand stroked him stronger. "I know. I don't want to taste latex. Now hush so I can taste you. I've waited long enough to have you on my tongue."

His head dropped back onto the pillow. "Jesus, Cass. Keep talking like that and I'll explode before your mouth can cover me."

"Now it'd be pretty hard for me to talk with a mouth full of your cock."

"Christ! I love that mouth of yours."

"Tell me that again when I'm finished here."

With lips still heated from his kisses, she covered the wide tip of his cock, stretching over him slowly. She wanted to savor this moment not just for the intimacy it presented but for the connection to Daren. Right now, she was the only one that mattered to him. With his cock in her mouth, he would be thinking only of her. For once in her life, she had Daren's complete and undivided attention. She'd be damn sure to make this last as long as her mouth could tantalize him.

The salty remnants from his earlier cum still clung to his skin, awakening her taste buds to dance with his essence. God, how she loved the flavor of him. Her tongue licked up and down his shaft like he was the naughtiest lollipop. A low guttural moan escaped his lips when she took him deeper. His thick cock gave her mouth a decent workout, stretching it, filling it.

Her fingers circled his cock at the base where it grew from a soft mat of dark brown curls. She removed her mouth long enough to adjust her position, taking the chance to inhale deeply, his musky scent mixed with her arousal.

Straddling his legs, she bent and flicked her tongue across the tip of his cock. Pre-cum pooled near the slit, offering a glimpse of his excitement. When she lapped it away with a hard, long stroke and ran her tongue along the thick vein, Daren practically shot out of the bed. Pleased with her ability to drive him wild, Cassandra concentrated on that area. Shock tore through her when he quickly fisted his hand in her hair, strategically angling her head to take more of him. She wasn't scared of how quickly he took control and maneuvered her head where he wanted it. She was stunned at the thrill that shot through her body straight to the core of her pussy by his simple, silent command.

But encouragement she didn't need, since she'd dreamt a thousand times of what he'd taste like and she'd guessed right. He tasted like an ancient god, hot, strong, and all male. His salty cum glistened on the tip of his penis for her to sample.

Daren used the hand entangled in her hair to move her head up and down. She allowed the caveman-like gesture for the heat it developed in her pussy. There was minimal pain to having her hair held in such a rough way, but pleasure abounded. Her body was alive with need. The need to touch, taste, stroke and the need to be touched, tasted, and stroked. God, this was incredible.

"Suck my cock, Cass. Yeah, baby. Suck my cock."

She swallowed him as deep into her mouth as she could take his massive cock. The soft pubic hairs tickled her nose as she brushed against them while burying him in her mouth. She felt so powerful. No doubt he was physically stronger than her, but right now she possessed his fragile control. It was up to her to drive him to the edge and give him the climax his body begged for. That power was addictive, aided by his approving moans.

"I love fucking your mouth, Cass, baby. This is so fucking good." His breathless compliments were music to her ears.

Pulling her mouth free, she took a moment to give her jaw a much needed break. Her tongue lapped at the tip, slurping the pearly drops of his pre-cum, and her hand worked jerkily up and down his shaft to urge the male essence from his balls to whet her appetite. She could feast on him all day and never get her fill. Her mouth took him even deeper. Moving her head up and down, she sucked relentlessly, her lips tight against his thickness as she worked to make him wild. She wanted him to explode with her name on his lips.

Every muscle in his body was hard and rigid. His hand in her hair had tightened as his hips jerked toward her face.

"Christ! Don't stop. Baby. I'm going to come."

55

"Mmmmm," was all she could offer since her mouth was filled to the max with his vibrating cock.

He loosened his grip on her hair. "If you…don't want…me to come in…your mouth…pull back. Now!"

She kept his cock inside her mouth and continued to move her lips up and down the entire length, sucking the head hard. Energy sizzled around them, his body heated to blistering. Her pussy clenched with the jerking movements of his hips as he drove himself to climax.

When his body tensed and straightened, the salty flavor filled her mouth. Quickly, she took him as deep into her throat as she could. Hot jets of semen spurted against the back of her throat as he cried out, his hand tangled deep in her hair. The pain was erotic as he held her onto his cock until he spewed every last drop of the salty fluid.

Licking her lips up and down the length of him, she left his penis glistening and replete.

"That felt so fucking good. You have no idea," Daren said, his voice strangled.

Oh, she had a clue.

"I owe you a bit of pleasure in return, baby," Daren announced, catching her arm to haul her to the top of the bed and switch places with her.

She laid her head back on the pillow while he sat near her hips.

"What are you planning to do to me?" she purred, her body already feverish imagining the wicked things he would do.

"I plan on watching you pleasure yourself. See how good you are at it." He leaned back on his elbow so his face was even with her hips. Talk about a front row seat!

"You want me to what?"

His smile creased his face and reached his eyes. His hand guided her legs apart giving him a perfect view of her pussy. A warm blush covered not only her face but her entire body.

"I want to watch you masturbate, Cassandra. Look at how wet your sweet pussy is. The juices are flowing over those soft, bare lips."

Oh. My. God. She was going to combust.

"Run your fingers over your pussy, Cass. Do it now."

What was it about the command in his voice that was such a turn on? Whether it was his tone or the gleam in his eyes, she didn't know, but her fingers inched down her belly to part her lips between her thighs and stroked.

"Like that, Daren?" she teased, watching his eyes fixate on her fingers.

"Yes, baby. Perfect. Insert a finger inside that hot pussy. I want to watch you finger fuck yourself, hard and fast."

She did as he requested, her pussy greedily slurping at her finger. The sensations pouring through her body were magical. Never had she'd done anything so intimate in front of another person. Never had she imagined herself doing this. And yet, with Daren, it felt so natural, so erotic. She kept her eyes on him and received just as much pleasure watching him enjoy her show as she did from the clenching of her vaginal muscles.

A moan escaped her lips without warning as the tension built quickly in her womb. Her fingers moved from her vagina to her clit and, applying firm circles onto the hard nub, an orgasm slowly developed.

"I wish you could see how sexy you look right now. Damn! This is so hot. Keep working that clit. Harder, Cass. Harder."

Her body trembled. Her lungs couldn't get enough air. But she didn't care. This felt too good to care about anything other than keeping her fingers moving over her clit.

"Come for me, Cass. You deserve it after your pretty mouth pleasured my cock so well. Come."

His commanding words pushed her over the edge as her hips lifted to meet her fingers. She cried out as her pussy quivered from the ripples of the orgasm, each wave pulsing from her clit to her womb.

"So pretty, Cass. So hot."

When his head bent and his tongue swept along her bare pussy lips, she yelled out. "Daren!"

Another powerful wave slammed into her body, robbing all strength from her body. Smaller waves continued as his mouth worked along her pussy until her juices were devoured. She barely had the energy to keep her eyes open as he lifted his head from between her legs, his lips wet with her juices, his smile wide.

When he moved to her, Cassandra fell into his embrace and allowed him to pull her beside him. He shut off the light before tugging the covers up over them.

Cassandra snuggled into Daren's strong hold, her head lying on the soft dark curls of his chest.

"Cassandra?"

Sleep was quickly taking over her exhausted body. "Mmmmm."

His lips rested tenderly against the top of her head. "Happy Birthday, baby. Hope all your wishes came true."

Chapter Three

When Cassandra awoke, she was alone in the bed. Before her heart could break, thinking she'd been abandoned during the night, Daren suddenly appeared in the doorway. He was freshly showered and shaved, dressed in clean clothes, with a cup of coffee in his hand. Did he have an overnight bag with him? Seems he planned last night very well, she thought as she stretched like a lazy cat.

"Morning, sleepyhead. Time to get up. Pack a bag. And bring your vibrator."

She sat up and stared, her jaw hanging open.

His grin was wicked. "Don't look at me like that, Cass. I know you've got one. I heard you use it the night I slept over last winter during the snowstorm."

When she found her voice, she spoke slowly. "You heard? Jesus! Why didn't you tell me—no forget I asked. I realize why you didn't tell me but, oh God, how embarrassing." She hid her face in her hands.

He sat on the side of the bed and caressed her naked breast, paying close attention to her erect nipple. "Why? It was the most erotic thing I'd ever heard. The constant buzzing of the vibrator, your soft gasps, trying not to cry out."

Narrowing her eyes, she studied his face. "How

could you hear that from the couch?"

He hesitated, but then spoke. "I didn't. I was standing at your bedroom door when I heard you pleasuring yourself."

She gasped and remained silent not knowing what to say.

Daren stared, his eyes growing cloudy with lust. "I've dreamt of that night so many times over the past year. I may not have been able to see you, but I only had to close my eyes to envision what was going on behind that door. I pictured you lying in the middle of the bed, your knees opened wide, no panties, your nightgown bunched up around your waist. Baby, I get hard just thinking of it."

"Wow, Daren. I never knew."

"I could see your fingers moving over your pussy, parting the lips, your juices glistening around the pink folds of your cunt. I imagined you using two fingers to open the clit to rest the vibrator against it. I swore I could smell your musky arousal through the door. Your soft gasps turned into harsh breaths after only a few minutes. I pictured your fingers sliding in and out of your pussy, your hips bucking for more depth, the vibrator humming against your clit. I pictured your fingers covered in your sweet cream. I could hear the soft slurping sounds as your fingers thrust in and out of your wet pussy."

"Oh my God, Daren."

His voice was firm, excited. "I leaned my ear against the door, desperate to hear your moans. While you were fucking yourself with that plastic toy of yours, I leaned against your door giving myself the best hand job of my life. All I could think of was how my cock would slide in and out of your cunt if I were in that room with you instead of your vibrator. I stroked the length of my cock until my cum erupted in long, hot streams onto my stomach. I came so hard my body shook for hours after. The last thing I heard before moving away from that door was you call out my name. I thought for sure I'd heard wrong. Fuck! I couldn't sleep knowing you'd just fucked yourself to orgasm and I got to hear it."

Completely mortified, she gasped. "You heard me call out your name during an orgasm and you never confronted me?"

"I figured it was the wine. My ego wasn't big enough to actually believe you really meant to orgasm thinking of me."

Her face flamed. "I can't believe you heard all that."

Daren studied her intensely. "I couldn't stand that you were only feet away from me, lying in your bed, dressed in that mouth watering silk nightgown. And because we'd finished off that bottle of wine, I felt rather indulgent and had marched myself to your door fully intending to sneak into your room, nuzzle up beside you and fuck you silly. Of course, only if you agreed." His smile spread from ear to ear.

Shock consumed her. "Oh, no. You mean, you thought about having sex with me last winter and I screwed it up by getting myself off?"

"Honey, I've wanted to have sex with you since you gave me my first boner in eighth grade swim class."

"I never knew that."

"You probably never knew a lot of things about

me."

Her lips curved into a feline grin. "I never knew I had that effect on you, Daren. I mean, you never said anything to me." She punched at his arm gently. "Damn it! Why didn't you tell me how you felt?"

He shrugged. "We're best friends. Our friendship means a lot to me. Plus, I didn't want to be like every other asshole that banged you, then got his heart broken when you tossed him aside."

Her mouth formed an O. "I don't toss men aside." Maybe she did, but not for the reasons he thought.

"Bullshit. I've seen you do it. Come on, Cass, this is me you're talking to. You like your men to fuck you good, you've told me so yourself. But as soon as their hearts get involved, you send them packing. I didn't want to end up a statistic."

How could she admit that she'd never become seriously involved with a man because none compared to him? Sure they were testing the boundaries of their friendship with sex, but admitting that she wanted more would send him running in a heartbeat. Best to give him time to adjust to their new intimacy. Then she'd confide her true feelings.

"If you believe that, then why change your mind now, Daren? Why choose now to fuck me?"

Sighing, he played with a strand of her hair. "Because, well, I've decided to accept an offer from my dad. I'm leaving to expand our ice cream company into New Hampshire. So you won't have a chance to send me packing because I'm already on my way."

Did she just hear him right? Sitting up higher in the bed, she raised her voice. "You son of a bitch! You fucked me without telling me you were leaving?"

His face was serious. "Actually I meant to tell you when I arrived last night, but then we started talking about the spanking and, honestly, that was so much more interesting."

Her heart disintegrated into a thousand pieces. He was leaving her. "You're an asshole, you know that?"

"Why? Because I'm moving?"

His words had slammed into her like an armored vehicle. She was flattened and lifeless.

"No because you weren't honest with me."

"So you wouldn't have fucked me last night if you knew I was leaving?"

"Maybe not."

"Don't give me that. Why the hell not? We were both turned on."

Is that all it was to him? Just sex? Not passion or desire? "So what? I don't make a habit of fucking every guy who turns me on."

"We're best friends sharing some great sex. Don't ruin it. Let's enjoy this weekend." He captured her hand and held it firmly, his fingers caressing her knuckles. "Tell me you don't want to use my body, babe. I'll leave now and we can forget last night ever happened."

He'd walk away from her just like that, wouldn't he? Oh, why hadn't she seen this coming? She should've known there was a reason behind his sudden sexual interest. She should've expected something to explain his pursuit of her last night. No man went out of his way to make her feel that special without an ulterior motive. This was an opportunity for great sex and he'd acted on it. That was all.

He'd ripped her heart from her chest. The pain

unbearable. The shock of his declaration hit her like a tidal wave, drowning her and her dreams with it. He would move away, take his friendship and leave her alone. All of her fantasies would go with him. Her love for him would remain as a constant reminder of what she'd lost.

What would he say if she told him how she really felt? Would he want to try their luck at a relationship? See if he fell in love with her too? It could happen over time. And with great sex it could happen sooner. Would he change his mind and not move away? Oh, hell, who was she kidding? She could never tell him her true feelings. He'd laugh and not take her seriously. The thought was just too humiliating. She forced it from her mind and bit her lip to fend off the tears that threatened to spill down her face.

"You want to forget last night never happened, Cass?"

Time to be the best actress of her life. "I'll never forget last night. Not after those mind blowing orgasms and that hotter than hell spanking." She was grateful there wasn't a hint of sadness in her voice.

His grin was devious. "Good. Then I propose we enjoy some more great sex while we can. Give me the weekend to show you how great fucking can be when you try things outside the norm. Let me share my sexual needs with you."

Her heart broke. "Just the weekend?"

"Exactly. We'll have the entire weekend to enjoy each other's bodies. I'll have you back in time for work on Monday. Promise."

She didn't want Monday to ever come. "I guess that sounds like fun."

"It'll be much more than just fun."

She ran her fingers up his arm. "Guess I need to get my fill of you before you leave. Hope you're up for the challenge." And maybe find a way to keep you from moving.

"Bring it on, babe. Just don't tease me unless you're sure. I don't play games unless they involve handcuffs and a paddle."

"Then it's a good thing being tied up is one of my fantasies."

He laughed. "You know, New Hampshire is only a few hours from Connecticut. Whenever you get the urge to fuck me, all you have to do is come up. And of course, I'll be back to visit the family too."

There was the devastating declaration she didn't want to hear. He just wanted her for the sex. Nothing more. She feigned a slight smile, words escaping her.

"Since I have another hard-on, Cass, let's make use of it in the shower."

She resigned herself to enjoy the moment. "I guess I should've put that on my list."

"No need to, babe. I've got it on mine. We'll multi-task. You need a shower. I need to fuck. We'll combine them," he said, leaving no room for argument.

With a quick swoop of his arms, he had a very naked Cassandra snuggled against his chest. Her hands clung to his neck. He carried her into the bathroom and set her feet down on the soft blue throw rug. With his arm securely around her waist, Daren leaned over and turned on the shower, testing the water with his hand.

"Will you let me bathe you, Cass?"

Her eyes opened wide. Did she hear him right? "What?"

"It'd give me great pleasure to bathe you. I'll soap your pretty skin, lather it nice with thick bubbles, then smooth it away under the stream of the water."

She laughed, her hand covering her belly. "Really?"

His expression became serious. "It's part of what I like to do, Cass. I promised not to laugh at anything you told me. I'd hope you'd return the favor when I share a part of myself."

Wasn't she a jerk? "I'm sorry. I certainly wasn't laughing at you, Daren. It's just that no one has bathed me since I was a little girl. I never thought of it as foreplay before now."

His hand circled the nape of her neck, drawing her lips to his. Steam filled the room, the sheer clouds dancing around their limbs. His lips were a whisper away from hers, but his hand held her head firmly out of reach. "Trust me to take care of you, Cass. Let me dominate you like I need to. Like I want to. Like I've dreamt of. Cass?"

Every cell in her body was charged and humming with fire. How she wanted to give herself to him like he asked.

"I don't know how to give you what you want, Daren. I've never had this kind of sexual experience."

"That thrills me to the core of my being. Knowing that I will be the first man to have dominance over you, Cassandra. The thought alone has my cock hard and ready for you."

His lips brushed over hers, not hard, but it was a possession just the same. Those hard lips covered hers, seeking her warmth and devouring her taste. She searched within herself for any sane reason to deny this wonderful man that she secretly loved the passion he'd asked her for. She couldn't find any reason to deny either of them the obvious pleasures they could share with each other. So what if Daren's ways of loving weren't conventional. He'd been the only man to sexually satisfy her, reaching her very soul.

Her hands lay flat on his rippled chest, the sharp thumping of his heart beat against her fingertips. "I want to try to be your submissive, Daren. I want to learn about it. I may suck at it, be warned. I tend to complain when I can't perfect something. I promise to try. But you have to promise to be a patient teacher."

His smile was wide with a hint of danger. "First lesson. Subs don't tell their Doms to do anything. The Dom tells the sub what to do. Understood?"

She blew out a breath. "Fine. But if you think I'm calling you Master, well that's where I draw the line."

He laughed and ran his knuckles up and down her cheek. "I guess it's a good thing for you that I don't go to that extreme. You won't have to call me anything except Daren. Lesson number two, disobeying your Dom will result in punishment. A punishment you'll have no say in and will not talk your way out of."

Her eyes widened as her pussy filled with her juices. Her belly did a delicious somersault. Never had a statement turned her on like that last one did. God, she may enjoy this submissive thing if it made her this aroused.

"Now, you can undress me," Daren said, watching her carefully.

Cassandra smiled. He was testing her to see how well she'd follow his instructions. Wanting to do a really good job, she concentrated on her task. Her hands tugged his shirt over his head and tossed it aside. Her fingers walked down his chest to stop at the button of his jean shorts. Slowly she squeezed the metal circle through the hole, unzipped the seam, and dared to glance at his face. He was watching her with an intensity she hadn't expected.

"Am I—"

He cut her off. "Subs must have permission to speak. If you ask nicely, I will allow you to speak freely with me."

She crinkled her brows. Now that was just unfair. She needed permission? "May I speak freely?"

"Yes."

"Am I doing this the way you want?"

The brown depths of his eyes darkened with carnal lust. She didn't need his words to know the answer, his nod was enough. Proud of herself, she continued.

She purposely went slow, allowing her fingers to linger along the muscles of his abs, watching as his breaths increased. She used her palms to guide the jeans over the hard muscles of his thighs and legs, holding the material as he stepped out of the fabric.

"Remain kneeling, Cass, while you remove my briefs." His voice was deep and firm, hinting of an underlying need.

She looked up to see him standing with his arms folded across his chest, a stern look on his face. Okay, so maybe this wasn't a time to smile. Cassandra did as he said and stayed kneeling, thankful for the small bathroom rug to cushion her knees.

"Lean up while kneeling, so your back is straight."

Her hands inched up his legs. She dug her fingers into the tight elastic waistband of his white briefs and tugged down. His cock sprang out to stand at a ninety-degree angle in front of her face. No wonder her wanted her kneeling for this.

"Very nice," she murmured.

She looked up in time to see his grin before he became stern again. He offered her his hand and pulled her up. She admired his wide shoulders, narrow waist, flat abs. Darren was a delicious piece of eye candy, no doubt.

Her hands flattened over his chest, her fingers toying with the soft mat of dark brown hair that lightly covered his skin.

He grabbed one hand and kissed the knuckles. Keeping her hand in his, he stepped into the shower first and put his back into the spray of water. Tugging her in, he held her closely in front of him.

"Tell me what you want me to do, Daren."

"Nothing. You just stand there and let me ravish you with my complete and undivided attention."

His lips found the curve of her neck under her ear and sucked. His tongue slipped out to apply long strokes up and down her sensitive skin.

"Mmmmm. I could get used to this."

Daren spun them around gently to change places, so that she was under the water. She was forced to close her eyes, but his presence was all around her. Her hands remained on his chest to keep her balance. She knew when his arm stretched behind her for the shampoo. She moaned when he began shampooing her hair, his long fingers massaging her scalp in small circular motions. Then he continued the same delicious treatment as he rinsed the suds from her long hair.

When he applied the conditioner, he took extra

care threading it into every long, curly strand. She didn't want him to stop. The lilac smell of the cream mixed with his musky cologne. She inhaled deeply, committing his scent to memory before the water washed it away.

Once again his fingers worked the water through her hair to rinse out the conditioner. His lips kissed her forehead, the tip of her nose, her chin, before settling on her lips. Her hands rested on his waist to keep her balance. The warm water sluicing over her body was heavenly.

Daren's tongue teased hers when she opened to let him in. Soft, slow strokes caressed the inside of her mouth before he pulled away and turned her out of the water to put his back under it.

Lathering up a huge bath sponge, Daren offered her a devastating smile before turning her around so her back was to him. With the soapy sponge, he drew circles over her back and down her butt cheeks, sliding into the crack moving up and down slowly. The intimate touch swelled her pussy lips until they ached.

His strong arm circled her waist as his hand skimmed the sponge over her breasts. The slow circles hardened her nipples, the sensation shooting down her belly into her womb. Her head fell back onto his shoulder, giving him access to her neck as his soapy hands glided up to her jaw line. With her eyes closed, she listened to the drumming of the water around them and inhaled the vanilla scent of her soap. Behind her, she could feel Daren's erection gliding against her lower back and ass as he sudsed her entire body. There wasn't an inch of her skin that he didn't clean intimately.

"Do you like it, Cass?" he said into her ear, his lips stopping to nibble her ear lobe. The sensation stirred her blood to a thunderous roar.

"Yes, very much. Don't stop."

He laughed and nipped at her jaw before talking into her ear again. "Just what are we going to do about your need to give your Dom orders. I'll have to punish you."

She laughed. "You sure as hell better." Then cringed. "Ooopss. Sorry. I did it again, didn't I?"

"Yes, you did, baby. You've earned two punishments now."

He turned her around, placing her back under the showerhead. His hands worked the water over her body to float the suds away. Everywhere he touched her skin, he left it sizzling and begging for his touch again.

"Cass?"

"Uh-huh." Her body muscles were relaxed, but her pussy was tense as the need to come grew fiercely within the depths of her womb.

His fingers slid between the soft folds of her pussy lips. Stroking, stroking, stroking.

"Oh. Oh, yes. Don't stop. I mean…that feels so good. Please don't stop."

"Now that's better, Cass. See. You're a quick learner." His voice hummed in her ear like a slow country song. Each word emphasized.

Under the warm spray of water, Daren positioned Cassandra's back against the wall. He turned away from her long enough to sheath his raging erection with a condom. His hand slid between their bodies to position his cock at her pussy entrance. She swore the steam around them came from the water hitting her heated skin. Her juices were already preparing her. She could tell by the easy way the head of his cock entered her. He grasped her waist to lift her against his body. With her legs wrapped tightly around his waist, he rode into her, his hips thrusting hard and fast. His strong arms held most of her weight, making the friction minimal from the slick, tiled wall.

This is where she wanted to be, held tightly in the comfort of his arms.

When he slid one hand down the crease of her buttocks and his finger prodded the puckered tight entrance of her anus, her body stiffened.

"Relax, baby," he said soothingly, his mouth near her ear. "I'm just using my finger for now."

"Sorry, but that's undiscovered territory. I changed my mind. I don't think I'll like that."

His eyes met hers, the softness in them melted her heart. "How will you know unless you try, baby? I promised you that I'd never do anything that I thought wouldn't give you pleasure."

His finger hadn't moved away from her anus, but it hadn't probed any further. The sensation of him touching her most forbidden spot was wildly exciting, a dark thrill.

"I believe that, Daren."

"Then you'll trust me?"

She breathed deeply, her body already enjoying the touch of his finger on that tight little hole. "I trust you. I'm just nervous."

He offered her the sweetest smile. "I understand. We're going to take this slow. If you don't like it, then I'll stop. You have my word."

"Okay."

His lips covered hers, his mouth warm and hard. He broke the kiss and leaned to speak in her ear. "You also have my word, Cass, that you'll soon be begging me to explore this tight little ass of yours. You're going to want me to take it like I take your pussy, baby. Hard. Fast. Deep. And often."

While he spoke those seductive words, his finger skimmed against her puckered asshole. There was immediate resistance so she clung harder to his neck. He drove deeper, spreading her cheeks with his other hand as he leaned her back against the wall to support her weight.

She cried out against the side of his neck. The sensation of his cock embedded deep in her pussy worked her inner muscles into a frenzy and the pain of his finger probing her butt hole was too much—she wanted to come now.

"Relax for me, baby. Take a deep breath. Focus on your pussy. Focus on the pleasures rippling in your pussy right now." He flexed his hips, driving his rod further into her heat and grinding against her clit.

"It hurts. Your finger hurts."

He didn't let her pull away from his exploration. "But you're not telling me to stop, Cass."

She must be insane to continue, but at some level she liked the feeling. "No. I don't want to stop yet."

"Good girl. Just let me do all the work. You concentrate on relaxing."

She mumbled a few curses into his neck.

He laughed and talked against her ear again. "Now, if I just heard you correctly then we're up to punishment number three."

She moaned as his finger invaded her a little more and his cock continued long, slow pumps. "Don't I get anything for good behavior? Like, a reward for being a good sport?"

He laughed harder. "I think you make a valid point. I'll consider that."

"Consider that I also must be insane for fucking my best friend in my shower while he sticks his finger in my ass."

"God, I love when you talk dirty."

His cock thrust hard into her pussy. She gasped as heat built inside her cunt walls, the thickness of his cock stretching her, consuming her. She'd lit his fuse and, like a stick of dynamite, he was ready to explode.

When he entered her ass up to his knuckle, her pussy clenched, the building orgasm only over the horizon.

She cried out. "Daren! Oh God, Daren!"

Every tiny muscle in the walls of her vagina and ass were dancing, like a flame hot and twisted. The explosion tightened her pussy around his cock, slowing his thrusts and making every stroke noticeable against her sensitive vaginal walls. She wanted him to remove his finger from her ass. No, that wasn't true at all. It felt way too good where it was. Why was it so hard for her to accept that she enjoyed this new form of sexual play? Because most consider anal play taboo? But now that she'd experienced a tiny bit, she wanted him to pleasure her, teach her more.

Her hands slipped off his wet skin, so she clawed at his shoulders, her nails digging into the hard muscles.

The water cooled, a welcome change for her

heated flesh.

"Oh, Cass, baby. You're so hot. I want to run my tongue along every curve of your body."

She couldn't respond. She was too busy focusing on how the burning and stretching pain in her ass could be so arousing. His free hand cupped her butt cheek, pulling her hips against his, his cock achieving a depth in her pussy she'd never felt before. The angle allowed the tip of his head to touch a spot deep inside her womb, each stroke from his cock sending a heated pulse straight to her clit.

The smell of lilac shampoo and vanilla soap twirled in the air to mix with the husky scent of their arousals. The steam caught each fragrance where it clung to the air to tease her senses.

Slowly, he used his finger to fuck her ass as he fucked her pussy relentlessly with his thick cock. His finger twisted in and out of her tight asshole up to the first knuckle then back out. The slow insertion and withdrawal was mind numbing. Before she could stop herself, her hips bore down on his finger, urging him deeper, faster.

"Tell me what you're thinking, Cass."

What she was thinking? Did he think she had a thought in her head with the wonderful tightness gathering in her cunt?

The water was definitely colder now. It refreshed her flaming skin but did nothing to cool down her pussy. No, the delicious climb to another orgasm was too hot to extinguish even with a glacier.

Her heart pounded so hard she could hardly breathe. "Daren. Don't stop. I'm going to come."

"I know you are, baby. I can feel your sweet pussy

tightening around my cock again."

"I can't do this. It's too intense. I can't." She didn't want to give up without achieving orgasm, but every nerve in her body was ready to burst into a flame. Spontaneous combustion would be the death of her she was sure.

His hips ground hard into hers, continuing to hit that sensitive G-spot deep inside. "Yes, you can. You will."

The pressure built first in her belly then spiraled out of control. Her nipples ached, her pussy swelled, her clit begged. With her eyes closed tightly, she willed her body to take that last plunge and release itself and give her the pleasure she so desperately craved. She willed herself to enjoy what Daren offered her.

"Oh, Daren. Please. Oh!"

He spoke through clenched teeth. "I…can only…hold off a…few more strokes. Come for me, Cass. Now!"

That rough demand, that Dominant tone, sent her arousal skyrocketing and igniting her orgasm like a torch. Pleasure ripped through her pussy as wave after wave of ecstasy over took every muscle in her womb, commanding her body to clamp around his cock and ride him hard.

His hips thrust into her, stilled, thrust again and stilled. His arms shook as his release spilled into the condom, his finger sliding faster and deeper into her ass.

There was no chance of holding off the next orgasm with her depleted energy. Her breath hitched as another flutter of spasms grew in her pussy and spiraled through her womb to her belly. Removing his finger, he massaged the tender puckered entrance to her anus.

She rested her head against his shoulder, his heavy breaths matching hers. His cock slid from her body as he placed her on her feet, keeping his hands on her waist for a moment.

"Legs okay to stand?"

"I think so." She lied. Her legs could pass for spaghetti right now. But she held her own and used the wall to lean on.

He discarded the condom and stood under the water to cleanse his semi-hard cock.

"Would you like for me to do that?" she asked, suddenly needing to give him the same attention he'd given her earlier.

He offered her a bright smile. "Would love it the next time, but this water is cooling fast and I have to finish bathing you."

"But you already did."

He lathered the sponge again and pulled her to him. "I saved the best for last, since I knew I was going to give it a good work out." He gently urged her legs apart with his thigh and placed the sponge between her legs.

She sighed at the intimacy. No one had ever made her feel like Daren was. Feeling like a queen, she closed her eyes and enjoyed his ministrations. He maneuvered the sponge over her swollen pussy lips, using his fingers to spread them wide so the sponge could access the entire area. Her pussy was heating up again to his touch and, if he didn't stop soon, she'd be begging to come. Not a bad idea except the water was getting chilly.

When he was done in the front he quickly wiped around her asshole. He dropped the sponge and leaned sideways so that the water swept away the suds, while his lips worked magic along the side of her neck.

"Did you enjoy yourself, Cass, baby?"

"Mmmmm. That was memorable, just like you promised."

He laughed loudly, reaching around her and shutting off the water. He stepped from the shower first to grab a large fluffy bath towel. Taking a moment, he wrapped her in it and helped her from the tub. He used another towel to dry her hair.

"Thank you for bathing me. It was a fantastic experience. Great foreplay."

He finished drying her hair and got a towel for himself. "Agreed. But don't think I've forgotten that you earned three punishments."

Her mouth opened, but he quickly silenced her with a finger over her lips.

"Make that two. Since you were cooperative with the anal play, I'm willing to forgive one punishment."

"Well, isn't that nice of you," she said unable to keep from being sarcastic. With her mouth, she would never make a good submissive. She just didn't understand how to *be*.

"Careful. Your tone could get you into deeper trouble."

Her belly did a flip-flop. Damn it. Why did it turn her on when he talked like that?

She walked into her bedroom with him. "So let me get this Dominant thing straight. I have to do exactly as you say or face punishment?"

"Yes. Pretty much. But—"

"And these punishments, what are they?"

He smirked. "That's the fun part. I call them punishment, but ultimately they're for your pleasure and mine. It's a way for me to control you by ensuring your pleasure."

"You're not making sense."

He toweled off as he spoke. "Punishment comes in many forms. Spankings and paddlings are one way. And you already know how arousing getting spanked is."

Her pussy gushed. "Yes."

"Holding off orgasm is another."

She gasped. "That's cruel."

He laughed, the sound dark and teasing. "You may think so, but being suspended in erotic bliss can be so pleasurable."

"I'm sorry, Daren. But I can tell you now that there's no way I'd do exactly what you say all the time."

He tossed the towel on the floor. "Not all the time, Cass. If you hadn't interrupted me earlier, I was going to say that I like to be Dominant sexually only. In all other aspects of my life, I want a woman who thinks on her own, forms her own opinion, and speaks her mind."

"That makes better sense then."

Pulling on his briefs, he spoke clearly. "I'm trying to explain it the best I can, Cass, but sometimes things are better experienced than told. So get packed and we'll spend the weekend showing you what I mean."

Wrapped in nothing but the large bath towel, Cassandra brushed her long, wet hair. "Why do I need

80

to pack? Where are we going?"

He tugged on a pair of shorts and a shirt. "I want to show you an amazing weekend. That's all you need to know. You're my sexual submissive for a few days, so you'd be wise to follow my directions. I promise, it'll be worth your effort."

She shot him a vicious glare. "And you'd be wise not to talk like that to me again. Submissive my ass." How could she admit that the thought of submitting awakened an erotic desire deep within her, thrilling her? She was a strong, independent woman who spoke her mind. She'd never be a good submissive. Would she?

"It's going to be your pretty little ass that suffers the consequences, babe. I can spank a whole lot harder than I showed you. Remember that," he said, his words playful and not threatening, but they held promise.

"Dominant or not, I don't see you ever spanking me in anger, so don't try to pretend otherwise."

"True. I'd never hit a woman other than for consensual spankings, but that doesn't mean I can't turn up the heat a little more and light your ass on fire. That is what a Dom does. Decides just how much a sub can take. It's my responsibility to make sure you only get what you can handle. That's why trust is so important. You need to trust that I will know when to stop, when you've reached that fine line of pleasurable pain before it turns to just pain."

Now he had her attention. "How do you do that? Is there some kind of training you take?"

He laughed. "No training, but there's plenty of books on the subject. A lot of it's instinctual. The other part is knowing your partner. Knowing what her limits are."

"Like when I tell you 'stop.'"

"Not necessarily. Some subs get so aroused they don't know they've reached their limit. That's why it's so important for the Dom to know when to stop."

Interesting. She had been very aroused. "I'll admit placing my trust in you did turn me on."

He sat on the edge of the bed to put his sneakers on. "Exactly. That's what it's supposed to do. By you trusting me not to hurt you, you're able to concentrate on your pleasure, enhancing it."

Choosing her cutest voice, she spoke shyly. "So since I'm so smart and a quick learner, does that mean I can get out of one of the punishments?"

His smile was mischievous when he stood. "Nice try. I told you, you can't talk your way out of them once I decide to give you one."

Her lips formed into the best pout she could offer. "What are the punishments then?"

He tweaked her nose with a knuckle before turning away. "Get packed. You'll find out later."

Cass crossed her arms, but resisted the urge to stomp her foot. "How will I know what to pack if you won't tell me where we're going?"

He pulled a slip of paper from his pants pocket and handed it to her. "Simple. Take everything on this list. That's all you'll need. You have ten minutes."

"What? You can't give me that little time to get ready to go away."

"I just did. Ten minutes and the clock is running, babe. If you make me wait, I'll paddle that pretty little ass again, and I promise that won't make for a comfortable car ride."

The smug look he flashed before turning and walking away made her fists clench and want to do bodily harm. Fine. She could get packed in record time. The jerk. She studied the list. Hell, with the few articles of clothing listed, she'd only need four minutes. And, of course, he listed her vibrator.

Purposely, Cassandra took fifteen minutes to meet Daren in the living room. She plopped her travel bags onto the couch as she offered him a bratty smile. She enjoyed the flare of lust that darkened his brown eyes.

He moved quickly, too fast for her to react. His hands latched onto her arms, dragging her up against him, and took her mouth in a kiss meant to void her mind of all sensibility. He tasted of coffee with the hint of mouthwash. She melted into his embrace, purring into his mouth. His tongue took her mouth with long, languid strokes. Every second his tongue fucked her mouth, her pussy got jealous. If he kept this up, she'd come just from his kisses.

Then panic struck. Oh shit! This was punishment. Not just a simple kiss. No. The way he was manipulating her mouth, sensually devouring her, was meant to arouse her. And it was working. But she'd bet any amount of money there'd be no relief.

When he ended the kiss abruptly, she had her answer. Her lips were deliciously numb.

Her pussy wept for his fingers, for his touch. And he wasn't going to give her what she craved, what he'd made her crave. The bastard!

He spun her around and landed five solid spanks to her skirt-clad bottom, his movements fast, powerful, and meant business.

"Hey. What the hell was that for?" she demanded

as she faced him, unable to resist the urge to rub her smarting bottom. She was shocked. Thrilled. Thoroughly aroused.

"That was one of the punishments I owed you."

"Oh? I thought it was for making you wait."

"No. Arousing you and holding back that orgasm you so desperately want was punishment for making me wait. I may have said I'd paddle your ass, but those beautiful lips beckoned me. I can change my mind."

"That's not fair. I don't like no orgasm punishments."

He smiled wickedly. "I warned you, baby. You knew to expect a punishment. Yet you still couldn't manage to get out here on time. I know you better than you know yourself, Cass. Thought you'd make me wait just to be spiteful," he stated, taking her bags and his and walking with her to the door. "Guess that backfired on you, huh?"

Chapter Four

They drove for an hour before Daren pulled off the highway onto a small two-lane road. His cock throbbed like it had its own heartbeat. He'd punished himself more than he had Cassandra with that kiss and the slaps to her ass. Damn, how he enjoyed spanking those beautiful globes. Her ass jiggled so adorably every time he landed his hand on them. And the heat from his hand print on her gorgeous ass was enough to make him come just knowing he had branded her, even if temporarily, with his imprint. Damn, that was so hot!

Shit! He had to stop thinking like that or his brain would lose blood flow from the never-ending hard-on crowding his shorts.

Cassandra stirred beside him in the passenger seat. Her car nap had given him time to consider what the hell he was going to do with her. There was no way in hell he'd be satisfied fucking Cassandra for just one weekend. He'd never be able to show her all the sensual things he could do to her body.

How could he make her understand they could be more than just best friends? How could he make her understand that this new intimacy didn't have to end after this weekend? He couldn't and that was the plain, sad truth. Cassandra was too set in her way to make any drastic changes to her life that weren't thought out months or years in advance. That last thought made him cringe because he knew Cassandra would be more willing to enjoy herself if she didn't feel obligated to take care of her parents when she had siblings that could help out.

Oh, but what he wouldn't give to dominate Cassandra and make her his sub.

Even though he didn't consider himself an authentic Dom in the true sense of the word, he did like to be in charge in the bedroom and all sexual matters. Cassandra's fierce independent streak would pose a problem. But isn't that what had attracted him to her? Didn't he see her as a challenge, a very sexy challenge?

And damn if his balls hadn't turned blue when she'd been so curious about the Dom/sub lifestyle, asking all those questions, while her eyes glazed over with lust and her face flushed with her arousal. It was all he could do to calmly answer her questions without bending her over and fucking her madly.

Daren glanced over, knowing they were almost to their first destination. He hoped it would be a pleasant surprise. He'd only really planned to tease her about a birthday spanking—a game, nothing more. He certainly never expected her to let him go through with it. The little vixen had made his wish come true when he placed her over his knees.

It wasn't really a game to him now, not after seeing those sexy little panties wet with her cream. God, he'd always dreamed of having her in his bed. Even those dreams hadn't compared to reality. Fucking Cassandra had been pure bliss. She'd lit a fuse deep inside him that was slowly smoldering. She was the oxygen to keep that flame going. Somehow, maybe he'd always known it, she was his breath of life.

Now he wanted to be hers. He had the weekend to enjoy her, maybe convince her they could be more. Maybe even a couple. How? He hadn't a clue, since he'd be living in Northern New Hampshire and she would be in Western Connecticut. Her family was here and she'd never dream of leaving.

But his family was in Connecticut too, and he was venturing to another state to start a new life, expanding his family's business, his livelihood, and his future. It could be done. Sure it was a little scary, change always was. Invoking his Dominant side wasn't an option. If Cassandra became his, then that had to be her decision and not something she perceived as part of a Dom/sub game. No, she had to come to him willingly or she'd regret it.

He at least had the weekend. Two days. Aw hell, he thrived on working under pressure, but this gave stress a whole new meaning.

Daren pulled into the Branded Fashion's parking lot and parked in the rear, farthest from the building. He had been to many adult toy stores but this one by far was his favorite because of all the variety of toys it offered. Sure he could've gone to any number of adult stores along the way, but he thought this one would be the most fun for Cassandra, give her an opportunity to browse hundreds of kinky items. And it was far enough away from their hometown that she didn't have to worry about anyone seeing her in an adult toy store.

Daren turned off the ignition and removed his seatbelt, depositing the keys in the front pocket of his shorts. Reaching over to where Cassandra still dozed, he ran a finger across her cheek, appreciating the softness of her flawless skin. She stirred, her eyes fluttering open as she straightened in her seat.

"Where are we?" Cassandra asked, adjusting her seat belt as she turned. "What are we doing here?"

"Do you really need an explanation?" he asked jokingly, pointing to the large pink neon sign advertising adult toys and videos for sale.

Her eyes widened and fixated on the flashing sign before turning to face him. "I'm not going in there."

He shot her a confident smile. "Yes, you are. We both are. How did you buy your vibrator?"

"At a friend's sex toy party."

"Now that I would've liked to see—you and a bunch of women drooling over the newest and coolest dildos. That must've been so hot."

He exited the vehicle, walked around the front, and opened her door. He released her seatbelt, then gently grasped her hand and pulled her out to stand in front of him.

"I brought my vibrator with me. There's really no need to go in there." Her normally confident voice cracked with nervousness.

"Nothing wrong with getting a few more toys for you."

She folded her arms. "No thanks."

His cock pulsed at her defiance. Her lips were set in a stern line and her eyes were focused on him. Hell, he wanted to fuck her right here.

"Didn't ask. Come on."

He appreciated the way her mouth opened in a small 'O.' With a smile, he took her by the hand and led her inside.

"Daren, I didn't sign on to be hauled around like a trophy."

After walking through the front door, Daren pulled Cassandra into a small room and backed her against a wall. Her shocked expression quickly turned to a heated frown, stirring his groin to even greater hardness.

"You promised me a weekend, Cassandra. I expect you to keep that promise."

She went to speak, but remained silent when he shot her a hard glare, daring her to interrupt him. His dark side was barely contained right now. All he could think of was finding some place to fuck her, to show her he wanted obedience now so he could give her the pleasure she deserved.

"You made a wise choice keeping your smart comments to yourself. This is what I want to do with you. I expect for you to please me by taking part."

"Thought you said you only played the Dom part in the bedroom?" she asked, her tone clipped. "Look around. We're in public."

His cock flexed painfully in his shorts. Goddamn woman was a Dom's dream. Around her, he'd stay aroused 24/7.

"I am a sexual Dominant, my dear. Bringing you here is part of that. I don't like to rule a woman's life, just her sexual pleasure. You will do this for me, Cass."

"Or what? Get punished?"

He grinned dangerously. "Glad you're finally catching on." He leaned so close his mouth was on her ear, his hands on her waist. "Disobey me here, and your punishment will have you begging to be spanked instead. I can, and will, hold off your orgasm for hours."

When she looked at him with lust filled eyes, he thought he'd cum in his pants. Jesus, he was getting drunk off her.

"Understood?" he asked, his voice left no room for argument.

"You've explained it quite clear, Daren."

If the little witch thought he missed her underlying tone of defiance, well, she'd be foolish. Smiling, he took her by the hand again and thought of ways to teach her about his Dominant ways as he led her to the first section he wanted to visit.

Slowly, they walked through the store; every wall displayed some sort of sex toy guaranteed to bestow the ultimate pleasure. Vibrators of every color and size sat alongside an assortment of butt plugs and dildos. Daren kept her in this section.

"Pick out three toys, Cass. If you can't, I will. But I hope you'd like some say about something you'll be fucked with later. I get to pick out my own toy and I choose these." He removed a package from the wall and handed it to Cassandra. He chose gold nipple clamps attached together by a thin chain.

She looked from the package back to him. "Wow, Daren. I knew you liked to be in charge, but why have I never seen this kinky side of you?"

He smiled wickedly. "Guess you didn't look close enough. It's not about kink. It's about exploring every way to pleasure my partner. I'm still the same old Daren you've known forever. Now are you going to pick out your three toys, or am I?"

She smiled brightly and sashayed up and down the isles. His cock was as hard as it had ever been, imprisoned painfully by the jean material of his shorts and begged for release from the constraints. Soon. Very soon.

Cassandra appeared nervous as she picked up packages, read them, and put them back. Looked like it was time to tutor her.

"Need help, baby?"

Her eyes glanced around them. "Um. I guess, wow. I never knew vibrators came in so many sizes and styles. Look at this one. It's not straight but has rings on it."

He took it from her and pointed to it. "That's to stimulate your pussy walls. There's many sensitive nerve endings there to give a woman immense pleasure."

"Mmmmm. I do remember that after having your cock stroking inside."

Fuck! He loved her dirty talk.

He handed the package back to her with a knowing look. "Why not get this vibrator? Then you'll see what I mean about the rings."

"Okay. Two more choices to go." She walked over to the display of spanking instruments and picked up a thin wooden paddle. "I do recall you saying something about paddling my ass."

He swallowed hard when she claimed the paddle as her second choice. Visions of using that toy on her naked ass danced in his head. He followed her until she stopped in front of the assortment of butt plugs. Hell, yeah. If she didn't choose one of those, he'd buy one anyway.

"So does this mean you're interested in more anal play, Cass?"

She sent him a cautious look before turning back to the multitude of plastic toys in front of her.

Damn, he was falling for her fast.

"Do you know anything about butt plugs?" he asked, loving how interested she was in all the toys.

Her cheeks turned a light crimson. "I know what they're for. I'm not naïve, Daren."

He raised his hands, palms out. "Sorry. Didn't mean to imply that. It's just that, well, you don't want to choose just any one. You're very tight so you need to start with a small one, like this."

He handed her a package with a bright pink butt plug.

Her eyes widened, the light brown depths fixating on the box. "There's no way in hell that thing will fit inside me."

When she would've placed it back on the rack, he simply placed his hand over hers and kept the package in her grasp. "That will fit perfectly. Trust me, baby."

"Trust you? Are you insane? It looks too wide."

He laughed because, even though she was being difficult and the Dom in him should take her to task for it, he couldn't. She just looked too damn adorable and truly worried. He'd forgive her disobedience this time.

His lips covered hers in what he hoped would be a soothing manner. But the heat searing through to his groin made him painfully aware that she tasted as good as she looked.

Pulling away, he kept one hand on her waist and the other over her hand and the plug. "This is the one we're buying. You must trust me. I have only your pleasure in mind, baby. This may look huge, but I promise it's the perfect size for such a beautiful little ass."

"Fine. But I don't believe you, Daren." She immediately rolled her eyes and bit her lip. "Damn it! What's that punishment one hundred? God, I'm sorry. I'm trying to understand the submissive role, but my mouth likes to speak before my brain thinks."

He kissed her forehead. "It's okay. I don't expect you to be transformed over night. It takes a long time for a sub to learn all the rules and adapt to the relationship."

They walked with their purchases to the cashier. At the counter, Daren grabbed a bottle of lube and waited in line.

"If there's not much we can do in a weekend, then why bother?" she whispered.

He glanced down at her standing very close to his side. She was so far out of her element. "Because this is who I am, Cass. Sharing myself with you—sharing my sexuality—means a lot to me. I want you to know the real me. Hell, we've been best friends for so long. Don't you think it's time you know all of me?"

"True. But it makes me nervous."

"What? Why?"

She shrugged. "I don't know. Maybe because I'm learning new things about myself, too. That's a little scary when you've lived your life one way and then suddenly start to crave something *else*."

His heart pounded in his chest. Did he hear her right? Jesus! "Do you really, Cass? Do you really crave more than vanilla sex?"

"I'll let you know after this weekend, Daren. I'm

depending on you to teach me all I need to know. Well, at least the basics. How's it feel holding my sexual identity in your hands?"

Christ! Like holding a live wire. "You're in good hands, baby."

He quickly placed their purchases on the counter and pulled out his wallet. When he looked up at the cashier, he noticed the heavily pierced and tattooed young man checking out Cassandra's ass as she pretended to read a porn magazine, obviously embarrassed to face the stranger. Daren smiled, knowing the man was out of luck. Cassandra was his now and he had no plans to let her go. He only hoped his seduction this weekend made her want a permanent relationship and not just a weekend fling. But he wouldn't give her the chance to break his heart like all the men before him. Daren planned to fuck Cassandra until all she could think of was him. Until all she needed was him.

Once the slow moving cashier finally handed him the bag and receipt, Daren took Cassandra's hand and walked out into the sunny parking lot to his car. He opened the car door, but stopped her before she sat down. He had her body completely shielded from prying eyes.

With his chest to her back and his arm around her waist, he whispered into her ear. "Remove your panties, Cass."

"What?" She wanted to face him, but his body held her in place. Only her head turned, her long, dark brown hair tucked neatly into a braid. Her light brown eyes opened wide.

"If you don't obey me, I'll bend you over the hood

and spank your bare bottom for the world to see. Or maybe I'll tie you in the back seat and leave the vibe against your clit on the lowest setting. Just enough for you to feel, but not enough to make you come."

She gasped as her body trembled against him. "You wouldn't dare."

He used his most authoritative voice. "I can see we really need to work on your understanding of the rules. Do not question me again. You will do this without defiance. I am not playing a game. There are certain things I expect from my woman and you will learn that."

"Or be punished," she whispered.

"Yes. I've been very lenient with you until now. If you truly want to learn about Dominance/submissive sex, including all the pleasures you could experience, then I expect no further arguments or debates from you. Make certain you understand that."

"I'm trying, Daren. I really am." She sounded shocked. "But you're asking me to, well, stop being me."

"No." He turned her around to face him, keeping his hands on her upper arms. "I'm asking for you to trust me with your pleasure. I would never change one thing about you, Cass. But, damn it. If you question and defy all my wishes, then this won't work. There are only so many punishments that can be given before it gets boring. And I would prefer to use my energy to pleasure you in so many erotic ways."

Her lips curved into a feline grin, causing his balls to ache. "I'm sorry. I do believe you requested that I remove my panties."

When he nodded and released her arms, she

hitched her fingers under her denim skirt and lifted it enough to give him a great view of creamy white thighs.

Under his watchful gaze, she shimmied her hips and moved the skirt higher and higher. The progress so provocative that his cock thrust forward, stopped only by his shorts. His gaze latched onto the sway of her body as the panties came out from under the hem of the skirt. Never had anticipation built so much within him. His pulse raged through his body, as his blood pooled in his groin.

Inch by inch, Cassandra edged the panties down her thighs to her ankles. He swore she purposely moved at a snail's pace just to tease him. He loved every fucking second.

The black thong panties shone brightly against her light complexion. When she bent for them at her feet, the denim skirt remained bunched around her waist, giving him a tiny glance of her bare pussy before she kicked her feet up one at a time to remove the thong over her heels. She tossed the discarded silk onto the floor of the car. When she lingered in front of him, but didn't adjust her skirt to hide her pussy, he was ever so grateful. The pink coloring on her face told him it had cost her to be so wanton. Her slight smile put him at ease. The last thing he wanted was to cause her any embarrassment.

Her arousal was evident as her breathing sped up and she shivered, in spite of the mid-day sun and balmy eighty degrees.

"Someone might be watching, Daren."

The parking lot, while not overly crowded, had a car enter or exit every few minutes. Daren and

Cassandra were in plain view for anyone with an interest to see, but Daren wanted to show her the most erotic pleasures and prove that no other man except him would ever do. He wanted to help her experience sexual play that she could only imagine until now.

"Do you trust me, Cass?"

She didn't hesitate this time. "Yes. I do."

His smile came quickly. "Turn around, baby."

She did so without argument, the curves of her ass coming into plain sight.

"Close your eyes and bend over the seat, Cass." He took the lube and butt plug out of the bag as he spoke.

When she did as directed and leaned her slender body over the passenger seat so her ass was sticking up, it was all he could do not to unzip and slide his throbbing cock deep into her wet pussy. Keeping his control, he fixed her skirt as high as it would go. The sun gleamed off the whiteness of her ass.

The only noise was the pounding of his heart in his ears and the whisper of the warm wind as it cooled his damp skin.

Tearing through the plastic packaging, he removed the butt plug and quickly inserted the batteries that came with it. When he turned it on, it vibrated against his hand. Hell yeah, she'd enjoy this so much. He turned it off again. It'd make her debut into anal sex so much nicer, so much easier to tolerate the invasion of his cock.

He leaned forward to whisper against her ear. Being this close to her ass and pussy, his cock had other plans. It throbbed painfully inside his shorts, searching for freedom.

97

"Cass, trust me."

With his knee, he spread her legs wide, keeping his hand on the small of her back to keep her leaning forward. God, what a sight her beautiful ass was.

His fingers were desperate to stroke her tight butt hole. It looked so inviting, so tender. He could barely contain his excitement. He was the first man to ever touch her asshole. His cock would be the first to expose her to the thrills her forbidden hole offered from an orgasm when her ass was being fucked. Just the thought made his cock ache miserably from being cooped up by the confining denim. How he wished he could whip it out and let her suck him until he spilled his cum down her throat.

He took a long, slow breath. Where was his control? He had never acted so desperate with a woman. Always, he had control of his body until the woman had been aroused just the way he wanted her. Never had his body been so damn commanding, wanting relief with an orgasm. His pleasure had always been contained with the utmost restraint.

Until Cassandra.

He grabbed the tube of lube and covered his finger in the clear slippery liquid. Taking a nervous breath, he stood behind her protectively. He glanced around to see if anyone was indeed watching, but there was no one. Imagine coming upon a scene like this. Normally, he'd enjoy such a public display, but where Cassandra was involved he wanted to protect her. He only wanted her to think she may be seen by others to enhance her excitement. His own arousal was heightened because others might witness him stimulating her body.

"This is just my finger and some lube."

He placed his slippery finger at the entrance to her anus. The puckered little entrance gave a hint of the tightness that lay beyond. Using his body as a shield, he moved very close to her, his legs bracing against the back of hers. His finger massaged the hole, instantly meeting resistance. He remembered how tight it had been in the shower, expecting no difference now. With gentle massaging circles, he enticed her to open for him.

"Cass, baby. Relax for me."

He felt her shudder under his hand at her back. Her lungs filled with air then slowly released. She relaxed only a tiny bit, but it helped. He slid past the puckered hole and stopped.

"Oh." Her bottom wiggled and then stopped.

"It's okay, baby. Your body will adjust as I go in deeper. Just relax."

"I'm trying. I'm okay."

Slowly, he eased his finger deeper and deeper. He closed his eyes and imagined that the finger was his cock and she was clamping tightly around him. A week ago, he'd never imagined sharing this kind of intimacy with the woman who'd been his best friend for as long as he could remember. A week from now, he couldn't imagine *not* sharing it with her. Hiding those worries in the back of his mind, he concentrated on pleasuring Cassandra.

When she wiggled and attempted to stand, he held her firmly on the seat, limiting her movements. Having this control over her was like being drunk. Nothing else in the world mattered at the moment. Just her pleasure.

Seated in her ass up to his knuckle, he stroked in

and out in leisurely movements, caressing her inner muscles, enticing them to relax. Her soft moans carried on the wind. His mouth watered with the need to kiss her beautiful mouth, to taste her. Gathering his control, he concentrated on the task at hand. He wanted Cassandra properly prepped for the next step.

Her body relaxed more and more as his finger met less resistance. He readied the bottle of lube and removed his finger, adding more of the slippery fluid before slipping two fingers into her ass.

"Daren! Oh."

His hand stilled and allowed her body to adjust once again to his fingers. "Relax, baby. You're doing great." He leaned forward to nip her earlobe while thrusting deeper into her ass. "Do you like it?"

"It's…different. But…yes…I think so."

Her husky voice filled with desire was all the encouragement he needed to continue with his plan. God, she was made for him. How the hell had he never realized this?

A quick survey of the parking lot showed that they still had plenty of privacy. "Are you wet, Cass?"

She groaned, but offered no words.

His free hand squeezed between her body and the seat to move across her belly and slide down to check how wet her pussy was and found her drenched. Her sweet juices flowed over his fingertips as he massaged her swollen cunt lips.

"You want to come, baby, don't you?" he whispered into her ear, kissing the side of her neck.

"Oh, God, Daren. Yes!" she said, straining to be quiet. Her hips bucked against the fingers playing with her pussy.

He finger fucked her ass faster and faster, both digits easing deeply into her without much resistance.

"More, Daren. I want more." Her soft moans thrilled him.

When her hips thrust back to force him deeper, he kept an even rhythm as he fucked her ass with the length of his fingers.

She protested when he removed his fingers from her ass and pussy. "Daren! No, please. I need to come. Please."

Her head swung sideways to look at him as she rested on her elbows. The light brown depths blurred with lust and need. Flushed with arousal, she was simply gorgeous. His cock flexed in agreement. God, how he ached to be inside her, but he needed to stick to his plan since the efforts of his labor would be rewarded later.

"Relax, I'm not done with you yet."

He generously applied the lube to the small butt plug and nudged it against her tight anal hole. His fingers grasped her hips to hold her still.

"Relax for me, Cass. Don't tense up. I'm inserting the butt plug. It'll help prepare your ass for my cock."

She gasped before she looked away again. He prayed she wasn't embarrassed. She had to get used to intimacy with him. The entire weekend, she would be fucked and pleased by him in more ways than she could ever imagine. The ideas he had for her kept him in a constant state of arousal.

He worked the plug past the tight entrance and felt her tense, her body becoming rigid. His other hand rested on the small of her back, gently massaging. "Ssshhh, baby. Trust me. You do, right?"

"Yes, but it feels weird. And we're in the parking lot. What if someone sees us?"

He smiled, but for her sake he glanced around again and, other than a few cars parked near the building, there was no one else around. "Then they'll be very jealous. Trust me to take care of you. I would never hurt you. Or embarrass you."

"I know that," she admitted. "Daren? Am I a freak if I liked your fingers in my ass? Because I did. I really liked that."

His heart skipped a beat. She was finally relaxing and trusting him. "No. You're not a freak, baby. You're beautiful and amazing." His free hand couldn't help but caress her ass cheeks, her skin so soft yet firm.

She wiggled her bottom back into the plug. Whether it was a natural reaction or her intention, Daren didn't care as long as he could get the plug fitted in her.

"Why do we have to use the butt plug? Why can't you put your fingers back in my ass?"

He laughed, thrilled she was enjoying herself as much as he was. "Because, baby. I can't drive while my fingers are up your ass, as much as I like the idea."

When she attempted to stand, he held her in place with his hand on her back.

"You mean I'm going to keep this thing in me? While you drive?"

He guided the plug in another inch and held it. With the widest part of the plug yet to be inserted, he waited to give her body plenty of time to loosen and accept the invasion of the pink plastic. His free hand roamed from her back to sneak under her body and squeeze her breast.

"Uh-huh. That's my plan. You see, I want you nice and stretched for me to bury my cock deep inside this tight little ass when we get to my beach house on the Cape."

His fingers pinched her nipple, pleased when she rocked her hips back into the plug.

"Oh! Yes!" She let out a long moan. "So that's our destination? The beach house?"

Twisting the plug, he inched forward a little at a time, the resistance stronger as the thickest part entered her.

"Yes. We'll have a great weekend. Relax for me, Cass."

"Oh God, I'm trying. It hurts."

Her labored breathing struck right at his heart, but if she could just hang in there a little longer then the pleasure would be worth the bit of pain now.

"The plug's almost in. You're doing great. Bear down on it. That'll help."

"What? I mean…oh hell. Okay. I trust you." She gasped and sucked in her breath. Moaned then squirmed more.

He'd excuse her tone and argument this time. She wasn't used to the pain and it was bound to make her edgy. But looking at that pretty little ass made him consider bending her over his knee and paddling her.

When she did as he instructed and bore down, he quickly thrust the plug all the way in, past the last tight ring of muscles.

"Oh! Oh!"

He collapsed on her back, his arms wrapping under her waist. "Ssshhhh. Baby, it's in. That was so hot."

She squirmed and bucked. "It hurts. I don't like it. Take it out."

His excitement deflated. "Just let your body get used to it. I promise it will quickly."

Her voice was breathless. "No. I can't do this, Daren. I can't be what you want me to be."

He stilled. He whispered into her ear. "Just be you, Cass. Wonderful, beautiful you. Will you give it a few minutes? If it doesn't start to feel good then I'll take it out immediately."

She was breathing hard, fighting the pain and the pleasure. He needed to get her to relax or this wouldn't work. It was his job to know her limits and he prayed she could get through this because he sensed she wanted it. If she truly hadn't she would've fought him tooth and nail to take it out.

"Cass, baby, you now have your first butt plug in your very fine ass. It's so hot. I wish you could see it."

He held his weight off of her but remained close. His hands rubbed her back and shoulder, caressing her butt cheeks and upper thighs. Her breathing slowly returned to normal, her breaths not as harsh.

She was accepting the butt plug. His cock throbbed in gratefulness.

"Better, sweetheart?"

"Yes. You're right. It doesn't hurt as much."

He stood up and gently helped her stand. "It'll be worth it. Promise. Now feel this." He turned the switch at the top of the plug to start the vibrator and chose the lowest setting to ease her muscles but not make her come.

"Oh, wow. It vibrates, too," she said and laughed. Quickly, she adjusted her skirt to make herself decent and shook her bottom a little. "Definitely different."

He couldn't help himself when he yanked her hard against him and devoured her mouth. Seeing the plug slip that final few inches into her dark, untouched crevice had his cock throbbing with relentless agony. All he wanted to do was feast on her. Playing so intimately with her ass had every sexual fantasy dancing through his head. While his tongue challenged hers and his teeth nipped at her bottom lip, the warm sun beat down on their already heated skin. His mind played out scenarios of the positions he wanted to fuck her in…sideways, against the wall, bent over, on her back, on her belly. Christ! The list was infinite. The possibilities were endless.

Cassandra sank against him, her hands splayed over his chest, her nails scraping his skin through the T-shirt. It was all he could do not to bend her back over and fuck her.

With the will of one hundred men, Daren broke the kiss, leaving both of them gasping for breath. He quickly reached for the hand wipes in the back seat and cleaned his hands and then brushed a fresh wipe over her tender flesh to remove any excess lube.

"Daren. I want you." Her voice was determined, desperate.

He growled, his hand covering her breast. Pinching her nipple through her shirt, he felt her tremble. She was close to coming. Her skin was flushed, her eyes clouded. Far be it for him not to oblige a lady.

"Gonna come for me, baby. That pussy was so hot. So wet."

His hand slapped her ass hard, her moan telling

him she liked it. His lips fused with hers again, their tongues battling for control. His hand abandoned her breast to travel down her belly, lower and lower. His fingers skimmed up inside her skirt and found her pussy wet with her creamy arousal, his touch causing the engorged folds of her sex to spasm. He swallowed her cries as he pushed two long fingers deep into her cunt, making sure to use different fingers than he had in her ass until he could properly clean up.

Her hips bucked against him, urging him to fuck her harder, faster. She exploded, her body sinking into his embrace and her silky fluid flowing over his busy fingers. Pulling out, he flicked over her clit a few times and was rewarded with another powerful orgasm as she collapsed into his arms and sank against his body. Tearing his lips from hers, he held her for a moment, while his lips rested against her forehead.

God, she smelled so sweet, like a summer morning. Her skin, soft and smooth under his caress, had him envisioning her naked and writhing under his body. For now, he just held her until her breathing returned to normal and her body stopped trembling.

"Think you can stand long enough to get in the car, Cass?"

She shook her head and he laughed. Scooping her up, he placed her gently onto the car seat, remembering the butt plug sitting snugly in her virgin ass.

Once she regained her composure, she faced him as he drove down the highway. "I like your kinky side, Daren. I just wish I'd known about it years ago."

"If you had, would you have jumped my body?"

Her giggle tightened his stomach relentlessly. "I didn't mean it that way," she said, innocently. "I just meant that I could've learned about the darker side of sex from you a long time ago and been having way more fun than I have been."

With other guys. Fuck! "You didn't strike me as the type to like bondage and discipline."

She squirmed in the seat. "I'm not a prude, for Christ's sake."

He signaled to change lanes and drove around a slower car. "You've also never dated anyone like me who is clearly a sexual Dominant. In fact, you've never dated anyone seriously."

Silence filled the car for a few minutes before Cassandra began the conversation again.

"Why do you have to move away? Why can't you expand the company in Connecticut and stay?" she asked, looking out the window.

Ah. Good change of subject. Don't answer any questions about a serious relationship. Yeah, that was Cassandra.

Staring out the windshield, he ignored the ache in his heart. He didn't want to move away from her. "Told you. I've been selected by my dad who, as chairman of the family company, is my boss. He tells me where I work. He got a great deal on the New Hampshire site so that's where I'm needed."

Her head whipped around to face him. "But why you? I mean you have two brothers who also work for him."

He laughed. "Yeah, and both brothers are happily married with two point two kids. No way in hell would my dad give this job to either of them and have his grandchildren move away. So I need to go to New Hampshire and build the next segment of the Hughes

Ice Cream empire."

"I know what it's like to be the only child a parent depends on even when there are other siblings. Hell, sometimes I wonder if my parents forget they have other kids since they only call me to run their errands. The excuse if that my sisters are busy with their families or hobbies. Wish I had time for a damn hobby."

"I'll be your hobby for this weekend," he obliged.

Her voice was soft, the concern evident. "But you don't have to move there. Not permanently, right?"

His hand gripped the steering wheel a little harder than necessary. "Afraid so. He's made me CEO of the New Hampshire site. I've always wanted to be my own boss and, even though I'll still report back to Pops, I'll have complete authority over the operations of that factory. So I have no option but to live there. It's a daily job and I need to be there for it."

"Oh." Her voice was barely audible. "Well, I'm proud of you. And happy for you if that's what you want."

You're what I want. "How come I hear a 'but' coming?"

She shrugged. "I'm going to miss you is all. We finally get together, have great sex. No, not just great, the best damn sex I've ever had, and I only get you for a weekend. It's not fair."

He held her hand, skimming her knuckles lightly with his thumb. "Come with me, Cass. Move to New Hampshire with me. Then we can still have great sex and lots of it."

Her wide eyes stared at him. "What? I can't do that. Maybe I can visit on weekends some time."

He frowned. "No, Cass. I want you every day. Don't you want me too? You just said we finally got together. Now do something about it. Come with me."

"I could only do weekends. My life is in Connecticut."

"The ride one way to where I'll be in New Hampshire is almost five hours, Cass. That's not taking into account inclement weather or traffic. It would be too much to drive up and back on weekends. For both of us to do, baby."

"You know I can't move, Daren. I help take care of my mother."

His sigh came from deep inside where his heart was aching with the idea of moving so far from her. "Your sisters and father can help with that and you could visit."

She blew out an annoyed breath. "My sisters help? I had to shut off my cell phone for this trip or they would've called me every five minutes to go do some stupid little errand that they were too busy to do for my mom and dad."

"So if you keep doing everything all the time when will they learn to pitch in and help? It's time for you to be too busy. Someone else will jump in to help when they're forced to."

She shrugged but remained silent.

"Cass, your mom is healthy now that she's recovered from her heart attack. If you're not here then your sisters will have to step up and do their share of your parents' care. Now any other reason you can't make a new life somewhere else? With me? The guy who's given you the best sex ever. Your words, remember?"

Why did she have to be so damn stubborn? Trying to convince her, sway her, he offered his best smile, hoping to ease her worries so she'd at least consider the idea before shooting him down.

Her once flushed complexion was now pale. "My life, my job, is in Connecticut."

With his patience wearing thin, he chose his words carefully. "Yeah, and you've talked a hundred times about leaving your dead-end job. How come you never have? Like when you got that job offer from your college roommate to join her in New York at that fancy accounting firm. You blew off the best opportunity of your life. And for what? To stay in Connecticut where your current employer couldn't give two shits about you?"

Her voice drowned out the soft music from the radio. "No. I never wanted to leave you, Daren. Okay? But now you're leaving me. Let's not talk about it any more. I'm having fun and I'd at least like to have this one weekend with you. Give me that, Daren. Please."

His eyes glanced from the road to her and back to the road. "Damn it. I'd give you a whole lot more, Cass, if you'd just let me. You said it yourself we have great sex."

"It's not possible for me to move." She cleared her throat, but didn't look at him. "I wish we'd done this a long time ago."

The smile she flashed him was fake, but he accepted the closure of their discussion, knowing they weren't done talking about her moving with him.

He winked. "Guess I always thought you were a good girl who wouldn't be interested in kink. But you're not a good girl, are you, Cassandra?"

When she placed her hand on his thigh and it journeyed up his leg to his crotch, he got his answer. Cassandra may not be fully aware of the sexual vixen hiding under her cool, proper façade, but Daren knew a wild woman when he met one. This new side of her made his balls ache.

She shook her head sending him a sinful smile. "Guess we're both learning a lot about each other."

Her fingers brushed across the outline of his hard cock through his shorts. It took all of his concentration to pay attention to the road. Firmly, her hand rubbed over the bulge with slow strokes meant to destroy a man.

His cock was desperate to jump through his shorts and into her grip.

She spoke too sweetly. "It's really too bad you're driving. I mean, if we weren't on this highway, I could enjoy a taste of you."

He growled. "Keep that thought, baby. I'll find a place."

Two minutes later, he swerved into the other lane and pulled off into a rest stop. When he parked far enough away to ensure privacy, he threw the car into park, rolled their windows down half way so they'd have air and killed the ignition.

Cassandra undid her seatbelt and climbed toward him. Her lips gently brushed over his, as her tongue traced the outline of his lips.

Pulling back, she looked into his eyes. "I wonder how long it'll take to make you come. Maybe I'll hold off your orgasm for a while. See how you like it."

He grinned, admiring her guts. "Try that, baby, and there'll be hell to pay. That I promise you."

Her smile tightened his gut. Didn't he have any affect on her when he displayed his Dominant side?

Her hands busied themselves with unfastening his shorts. He lent a hand by lifting his hips and yanking down the stiff material. His grateful cock sprang forward into Cassandra's waiting hand.

In the cramped space, she got on her knees and placed her head between his chest and the steering wheel. When her slender hand gripped his thick erection, he thought he'd come instantly. Instead, he dragged deep breaths into his oxygen-starved lungs and laid his head back against the headrest. Shutting his eyes, he surrendered to the soft sounds of her breaths and her pleasing touch.

As her fingers stroked up and down his shaft, her lips opened over the head of his cock, taking his thickness into the warmth of her mouth. Never had a woman's mouth felt so velvety, so sexy. He placed his hand at the back of her neck, his fingers massaging the soft skin with lazy circles.

"Oh, baby, that feels great."

Before he could speak any more words, her mouth closed completely around his cock and took him deep inside until the head hit the back of her throat.

"Sweet Jesus!" His hips jerked off the seat.

She eased back, moving that talented mouth up and down, taking him in and out of her warmth.

"I love fucking your mouth, baby," he said, breathless.

The air in the car was stifling even with the windows down. But he'd be damned if he stopped her so he could start the AC. Hell no. He'd sweat to death before he interrupted this delicious attention.

When she pulled her mouth free from his cock, he lifted his head and opened his eyes. Her tongue was licking her lips while her fingers strummed along his erection.

"Problem?" Please don't let there be. She had to finish.

"Enjoying it, are you?"

"Fuck yeah."

"Mmmmm. Good to know." She smiled and returned her mouth to his cock.

Christ, she made him nervous with that devious look. She was up to something. Her threat to hold off his orgasm lingered in his head. She'd better think twice about doing that, the little witch. That'd be challenging the wrong person. He was so much more well-versed in holding off orgasms than she could hope to be.

With her sweet mouth swallowing his cock once again, he closed his eyes and leaned his head back. "You do this like I dreamed you would. Yeah, I've had many nights filled with you in my dreams, baby."

"Tell me," she said, interrupting the blowjob long enough to say the two words.

If he could concentrate long enough, he didn't mind sharing his dreams with her. "I dreamt of how hot your mouth would feel when you took my cock into it. How those soft lips would feel sliding over my entire length. How that naughty tongue would touch and tease."

"Mmmmm."

His hips arched again, urging her to take him deeper. "Ahhh. Fucking yes. Not much longer. Fucking yes."

"Mmmmm."

With his eyes closed, he felt for her braid and wrapped it around his fist, holding her head against his cock. His balls were probably blue by now, his release just waiting to spill forward.

"I…dreamt of laying you down on your back and straddling your face. Fucking that mouth while you sucked me hard. Oh, baby. I'm so close."

"Mmmmm." Her lips closed over his hardness, while her tongue ran along the thick vein under his penis, driving him to the brink of explosion. She worked at a steady pace, taking him to the back of her throat and stroking him firmly with her small hand. When her mouth pulled back to circle the tip of his penis, he lost it.

His hips jerked forward, shooting his cum into her greedy little mouth. She swallowed and continued to suck until every last drop was gone. His entire body shook, every muscle tightened, aware of his explosion. His eyes opened wide, staring at the roof of the car. He eased his hand from her braid and released her.

Sitting silently, he breathed lighter since she no longer held his cock, but gently rubbed his inner thigh. The touch electrified his skin. He turned, facing the most beautiful woman he'd ever laid eyes on. He'd fucked many women in his life, but damn if he could remember any of them right now. He ran his fingers down her cheek. She grabbed hold of his hand, opened his palm, and placed a soft kiss on it.

The simple gesture moved him. He swore his heart swelled, a feeling he'd never experienced before. Must be the result of a fantastic orgasm.

Zipping his shorts, Daren glanced over at

Cassandra as she fastened her seatbelt, licking the remainder of his cum from her lips. Her tongue left a glistening trail.

Yeah, his stubborn best friend didn't know it yet but, by the end of the weekend, he wasn't taking no for an answer. Cassandra was going to move with him. There was no way a few days of sex would be enough for either of them. No way.

He had the entire weekend to convince her to join him in New Hampshire.

Chapter Five

Daren and Cassandra arrived by mid-afternoon at his family's beach house on Cape Cod. Her heart broke every time she thought of Daren asking her to move to New Hampshire with him. If only he'd asked her because he wanted her and not just for the great sex, then maybe she'd consider it. Her mother was recovering better than expected. And her sisters definitely could do more to help. But Daren had been honest from the beginning, so she couldn't fault him or hold his ideas against him. Who's to say a relationship between them would actually work. If it didn't, she'd lose her best friend and that would be too great a loss.

All Cassandra could do was to enjoy the weekend, while having awesome sex. That's exactly what she planned to do. There was no reason she couldn't enjoy Daren's body and live out her fantasies for the next two days. All she had to do was protect her heart. Just how, she hadn't a clue.

After depositing their bags in the bedroom, Daren held her hand as he led her to the bathroom. It was awkward to walk with the butt plug still in and she had to admit her ass was a little bit tender.

He towered over her in the good-sized bathroom. "I'm going to remove the butt plug, Cass. All I want you to do is rest your hands on the sink and lean forward a little."

She glanced at the porcelain sink then back at him. "Um, okay. Is this going to hurt?"

His lips kissed her forehead, the touch giving her goosebumps. "You'll feel pressure as I pull on it, but only for a few seconds. Turn around for me. I'll turn the vibrator off first."

The vibrator had been the best part. The silent hum in her ass the entire car ride reminded her of riding on a motorcycle. It was tantalizingly erotic, a constant reminder of what exactly was in her and why it was there, to prep her for Daren's cock.

She did as he said and leaned over. His hands lifted her skirt. The air hit her bare bottom, making her aware that Daren now saw her again as intimately as any guy ever had. She felt him grab the base of the plug, turn it off, and gently pull. His careful maneuvering of the plug did nothing to diminish the pinching feel of it passing through her tight hole.

"Oh, man!"

"One more second."

With a quick tug, he freed the plastic toy from her anus, the sensation of being filled leaving her with the release of the plug. She expected her ass to burn or ache, but was pleasantly surprised when she felt neither. All she sensed was an awareness of being stretched and touched. He kept his palm on her lower back and retrieved a washcloth from the rack behind him after washing the butt plug.

Watching him in the mirror, Cassandra admired his hard male body. Her pussy clenched, whether from the sight of him or from the relief in her butt hole, she didn't know or care. It felt wonderful to feel her pussy come to life again after her massive orgasm earlier.

Using the washcloth, he gently wiped between her ass cheeks, washing away the lube. His strokes were extremely gentle and the warmth from the wet cloth soothing. When he was finished with his task, he pulled her skirt back down and circled her waist with his arms. Looking at her in the mirror, he placed his lips on the side of her neck. Automatically, she tilted her neck, offering him what he sought.

When his lips suckled the sensitive column, she could have melted into the floor. Probably would've if he weren't holding her so tightly.

She wanted to protest when he stopped, but she remembered her promise to embrace her submissive side. So she'd let him call the shots for now, even if it meant he left her horny and very needy.

"How about a walk on the beach, baby? After being stuck in that car for hours, I think it'll do us good to get some exercise and fresh ocean air. No sense wasting such a beautiful day indoors."

"Sounds like fun," she agreed, following him from the bathroom through to the deck. "Of course, you forgot to add bikini to the list of items you wanted me to pack. I could've gotten some rays."

With a glance, Cass could tell he had no plans for sunbathing as his eyes roamed over her from head to her toes.

He opened the deck door and motioned for her to precede him. "No bikinis needed. In fact, no clothes will be necessary much of the weekend."

Her pussy clenched at the idea of spending the whole weekend gloriously naked in Daren's arms.

The sun was bright in the summer sky, its rays cascading off the water as small waves gently lapped ashore and washed over the golden sand. The Atlantic Ocean was calm as sea gulls flew feet above the water looking for fish. The private beach was isolated from its nearest neighbor half a mile on either side.

"This is so beautiful, Daren," Cassandra said, linking her arm in his as they walked onto the deck over looking the ocean. "How come you've never taken me here before?"

"Because I'd never want to let you go if I did," he told her simply. "I have this weekend to convince you to move with me to New Hampshire. I'm counting on the hot, wild sex to make my argument and prove to you the kind of sex life we'd enjoy if you joined me."

She was so confused. How could fate be so cruel to finally give her the man she loved only for him to relocate two states away and want her just for sex?

Sighing, she looked at her feet. "Life's not all about sex, Daren. What would happen if sex got boring?"

Laughter erupted from him. "With you? I seriously doubt that. But you wouldn't be chained down. If you didn't like it, then you could leave whenever you wanted."

Of course she could. He wasn't into settling down with any one woman. He'd never ask her to stay and be anything more than a sex partner. Damn it if she didn't like that idea so much. Who said she needed him to declare his love to be happy? Couldn't she be just as happy living near him and having great sex? A lot of women would love to be in her predicament. And a lot of married couples broke up. So what was so wrong with just enjoying the sex?

She knew why. Because she wanted the happily-ever-after bullshit and she wanted it with Daren. The blockhead!

Her heart shattered into tiny pieces, a physical pain akin to being kicked. "I know that. And you know I can't go with you."

He leaned back against the railing. "I don't know any such thing. I think you're scared and rightfully so. This probably seems rushed between us, which is my fault. I should've been more honest and open about my feelings for you before now."

You think? "Why weren't you?"

His expression was so serious that she wanted to capture his face in her hands and kiss him madly.

His voice was soft but strong. "I was afraid to ruin our friendship. You're the most important person in my life, Cass. I was so sure you'd reject the idea of sex between us that I never made a move. Although, I wanted to beat the shit out of every guy you've dated since high school."

She could do this. She could pretend all she wanted was the sex, too.

Her hand brushed over his cheek. "I think I need some convincing."

Leaning up on her toes, Cassandra pressed her lips to Daren's. His mouth opened instantly to allow her the access she sought. He tasted of mint and heat and she couldn't get enough of him.

His arms came around her waist, his powerful fingers digging into her sides. He deepened the kiss, his mouth overpowering hers, his tongue devouring her taste. She was high on love, addicted to his touch.

Then he broke the connection.

"I love kissing you, Cass. But if we continue, I'm going to fuck you."

She smiled. "I don't see a problem with that."

He returned the smile. "I know. But I want to walk with you on the beach. I have a whole night of pleasure in store for you. Your body needs a rest before I take you again."

"Aren't you the gentleman," she said, allowing him to take her hand and tug her down the stairs onto the sand.

"Hardly. Just looking out for my own interest. You wore that butt plug a while and your body deserves a rest. If we walk, the chances are a little better that I won't fuck you and your body will rest."

She kicked off her sandals and he removed his sneakers. They left them on the bottom step before walking toward the water's edge.

"So you don't plan on having sex with me on the beach?"

He growled low before he scooped her up and threw her over his shoulder. She screeched in delight.

"Keep giving me ideas, baby. Keep giving me ideas," he warned.

His hand smacked down hard on her ass, causing her to yell out. He gently placed her back on her feet and held her hand while they walked through the wet sand.

With the sun's rays reflecting off his thick, brown hair and his light brown eyes squinting, he looked the picture of male perfection. His hand held hers possessively, his strength obvious in the tight grasp. She glanced at him as they walked and appreciated the way his long legs strode in determined steps, his narrow waist molded by the snug shorts. God, she wanted to peak around and steal a look at his ass. She imagined it flexed nicely in the faded blue denim.

Curiosity got the best of her, so she leaned her head back and checked out his ass. Not disappointed at all, she smiled. Just like she expected, those firm ass cheeks flexed very nicely in those jean shorts.

Straightening out again, she cleared her throat. "Daren, can I ask you a question?"

"Of course."

"When did you know you liked an edgier kind of sex? I mean, how did you know you like to be Dominant in bed?"

The rise and fall of his chest caught her attention as she studied the outline of muscles under the T-shirt. Very nice. "It was in college. Had a girlfriend who let me try things with her no other girl had let me do before. Things that seemed to come natural to me."

"Like spankings and anal sex."

"Yeah. But non-Dominant men do those things, too. I was different. I sensed it."

"How? Help me understand this side of you, Daren. I mean, I've been your best friend all these years and I never knew about this side of you."

"Yes you did. You just chose to ignore it. Not question it."

Did she? Looking back she had to agree. She always knew he liked to be in control in the bedroom—hell he boasted about it—but she never inquired to what extent. Then again, she had no reason to ask since he'd never offered to give her a birthday spanking before or made any other sexual advances.

"Zoning out on me there, Cass?"

"Oh, sorry. Was just thinking. I guess you're right. I chose not to ask you about your sex life even when a part of me knew you were different from all the men I had dated."

"It was probably best you didn't ask."

She squinted when she glanced up. "Why do you say that?"

His profile was sharp, dangerous. "Because I don't think I could've answered your questions without throwing you down and fucking you. Told you yesterday. I've wanted you in my bed for a long time."

Her belly did little flip flops that rushed to her pussy. "Yet, you said nothing."

Wide shoulders only shrugged. "Of course."

If she wore shoes, she would've kicked him. "Well, you should've."

His head whipped sideways to glare. "I should've? What about you? You could've said something."

She huffed her breath. *Yeah, right.* "Oh, like what? Daren, I think you're so hot. Come over tonight and fuck me because I'm sure you're great in bed, from all the rumors I've heard."

"That would've worked."

The jerk! "See. It's stupid male comments like those that make me kick men to the curb."

His jaw tightened. "I'll consider myself warned."

The warm breeze coming off the ocean did nothing to cool her rising temper. "Maybe I wouldn't have let you fuck me. Ever think of that, Daren?"

He sent her a look that screamed, *oh please.* It boiled her blood.

She stopped and jerked her hand from his. "I'm

only allowing you to fuck me now because I'm in the middle of a dry spell and horny as hell." She didn't miss the dangerous gleam in his eyes, but continued anyway. "You're lucky it is great sex or I wouldn't have come for the weekend either."

"I'm glad we're having this heated discussion, Cass."

Of all the things he could've said, that was the last thing she expected. So standing there in shock was acceptable in her opinion, since she really didn't have a clue as to how to respond to such a stupid statement.

"Wow. That doesn't happen often," he said, sarcastically, his arms locked across his chest.

She frowned. "What doesn't?"

"You without a smart ass response."

Her fists clenched at her side. She wished she were strong enough to push him into the surf. That would teach the bastard a lesson!

Of course, then she would have to run like hell. Since she wasn't in the mood to do that, she abandoned the idea of sending him for a dip in the ocean.

But she could do the next best thing. Her finger jabbed him in the chest sharply.

"Tell me why you're so glad we're fighting, Daren."

When his lips curved into a wise grin, she did everything she could not to smack it off. Where the hell was all this temper coming from?

Facing her with his arms crossed over that wide, muscular chest, he towered over her. "Because at least this proves to you that I'm willing to let my woman speak her mind outside the bedroom. I told you that I only like being Dominant in the bedroom and when sex is involved. Otherwise, you'd be in a lot of trouble right now."

"Oh, really? Well, you don't scare me, Daren. And I'm not your damn woman. We're fucking for the weekend, that's it. Remember?"

"Clearly."

"I agreed to play this Domination game because we were having great sex. But just remember, I'll continue to speak my damn mind when I want to."

Cockiness seeped from every one of his pores. "Really, Cass? Because I don't think that's what you want. And I sure as hell don't think this is a game to you. It sure the fuck isn't for me."

"Don't get your hopes up too high. I'm not your typical submissive, so I won't live up to your expectations or needs for long. That's why just the weekend's good enough for us. We get to fuck off some of our lust for each other and then get back to our normal lives."

His hands grabbed her upper arms and pulled her to him. "That's where you're wrong, Cass. Being a submissive in bed is exactly what you are. Exactly what you want to be. Exactly what you need to be. Now just admit it to yourself."

"The hell I am."

"Told you before that there's nothing wrong with being sexually submissive. I happen to love the non-submissive side of you at all other times."

"I am not submissive."

"Then why does being one appeal to you so much? I'll tell you why."

She stared at him.

His head leaned down until it was inches from her

face, his voice calm and firm. "Because you need to give up control, Cass. You have control over everything else in your life…at work, at home, with your family, with your friends. It wears on you. So in the bedroom, when you can give up control to your lover, who right the fuck now happens to be me, you thrive on it."

Did he just acknowledge her as his lover and not just friends-with-benefits?

"What about you, Daren?" she shot back just as heated. "What makes you Dominant in bed? Tell me, because I want to know what drives a man like you—handsome and successful—to bed a woman then move on to your next conquest. Is that a Dom thing?"

This close to his face, she could see his jaw clenching, every angle of his handsome features was taut, rigid. "I need to be Dominant in bed because the rest of my damn life is either controlled by someone else, like my father who is also my damn boss, or something else, like my family business which is also my legacy."

Why she wanted to fuck him when they were having this heated debate was beyond her, only proving he was a potent man. "Then find another damn job," she yelled at him.

"It'd be the same anywhere I worked. I'd always feel controlled. So in bed, I like to be the one who controls the mood, the position, the whole fucking act. But most of all, I like to be the one to control the pleasure. You see, there's nothing like bringing my lover—you—to orgasm and giving her the pleasure she searches for. It's a natural aphrodisiac for me. I can't be anything different. Just like you can't be. So in a weird way, we're a perfect match."

Yeah, if you didn't consider the fuck-buddy arrangement and you weren't moving two states away.

"I'm sure you'll have no problem replacing me in bed."

"That's where you're wrong, Cass."

She stared at him. Wrong?

"You're the only woman I haven't scared away. The women I take to my bed barely last the night once they see my Dominant side and what I require in bed."

Her mouth opened wide before she spoke. "Are you serious?"

His long sigh would've broken her heart on its own. But it was the loneliness etched on his face that pierced her heart. "They all think it's sexy and fun and claim to be submissive. But once in bed with me, they think twice and end up leaving, if not that night, then the very next morning. They don't come back."

"I never knew." She never would have guessed he had trouble getting a woman to return to his bed. They all must've been insane to pass on a man like Daren— strong, handsome, insatiable.

He frowned, at least that was better than seeing him so sad. "How would you? I never told you. You can claim the record for staying in my bed the longest. It's been almost two days. Since you haven't indicated a desire to leave, then the night's looking good for me."

Her hand reached out in an automatic gesture to console him by running her fingers up and down his arm. "Of course it is. I'm having a good time with you, Daren. If I wasn't, I wouldn't be here."

His half smile was at least a start to getting him

back to a better mood. "I know, baby."

"Wow. We just had our first fight as lovers, didn't we?" she said and smiled.

His lips curved wickedly. "You know what that means, don't you?"

"What?"

"Makeup sex and lots of it." He scooped her up in his arms and twirled her before lowering her to the ground to lay his lips against hers. His long body crushed hers into the softness of the sand.

When he pulled away, she looked up at him. "Daren?"

"Uh-huh."

"I think I like being submissive. Of course, in bed only. Anywhere else would be near impossible."

"Agreed, my little devil."

His head bent again, his lips barely brushing hers when a child's scream harpooned through the air. They both jumped up to see a young boy screaming at his dog who was in the water.

"Daren, I think the little boy's in trouble," Cassandra said, nervously.

"Come on." Daren said and took off running toward the boy who was about thirty yards away. Cassandra followed closely behind.

"What's wrong, kid?" Daren asked.

"Philip is drowning," he said through sobs.

"Philip? Who's Philip?" Daren searched the water, his head whipping back and forth over the area.

The boy pointed at the dog in the surf and cried harder.

"Aw, kid, don't worry. Dogs love the water. He's just playing."

"Nu-uh. He's drowning."

Before Daren could debate the subject any more, Cassandra tugged his arm. "I think he's right. Look. The dog is struggling. Daren, do something."

The dog's head bobbed and then went under the water for what seemed an eternity before it broke through the surface and the dog paddled hard.

Daren cursed, stripped off his shirt and dove into the water.

Cassandra did her best to console the boy. She laid her hand on his shoulders. "What's your name?"

"Danny."

"Danny, where are your parents?"

"Down there at our house. Philip ran this way. I tried to catch him and then he dove into the water and now he's gonna drown."

The boy was inconsolable as Daren wrestled with Philip in the water. Waves crashed over the pair, as the dog clearly didn't trust Daren. The dog was large, but by the time Daren hauled him from the ocean the pooch had given up the fight.

Danny cheered and rushed from Cassandra's arms to hug Philip.

Daren breathed heavily, his jean shorts glued to his legs. Water streamed over his rippled chest, every muscle flexed and prominent. His thick, brown hair was messed and streaming water over his face. Cassandra couldn't tear her eyes from him.

"Thanks, mister. You saved his life."

Daren bent and picked up his T-shirt, shaking the sand off before using it to wipe his face. "Yeah, well, get him home and keep him on a leash from now on."

The boy and dog slowly trotted off.

Daren cursed again. "Stupid dog. Kept me from feeling up a hot woman."

"Awww. This hot woman thinks you're a hero."

He huffed a breath while he pulled on his T-shirt.

She ran her fingers up his chest. "I think my hero needs a nice massage after those heroic efforts."

He smiled. "I like how you think."

"I'm sure. Will you allow me to give you a massage? The submissive in me wants to please her Dom."

His smile was wide, his face softer than a few minutes ago. "I can't think of anything else I want right now."

Putting on her best sultry look, she set out to seduce him. "Oh, really?"

"Okay, maybe I could think of like forty other things, but let's start with that massage."

"Okay. But only if you beat me back to the house. Race you!" She took off like a bullet, her bare feet kicking through the sand.

"Damn it. I just saved a friggin' mutt."

But despite Daren's protest, he caught up pretty quickly, scooped her up by the waist, and swung her around so she could wrap her legs around his hips. Her hands wrapped around his neck as he slowed his pace to a walk.

"Isn't this much nicer?" he asked, cradling her tightly.

"Mmmmm." Her lips found his neck and sucked hard. That was the sweetest thing she'd ever watched a man do when Daren jumped into the surf to save a dog for a kid he didn't even know. She'd make sure to give him a hero's welcome once they got into the bedroom.

He growled, cupped her ass, and did double-time back to the house.

****

The woman was going to drive him insane.

Daren lay back on the bed, glad he utilized the outdoor shower to rinse off the salt water and sand because he wanted Cass's lips on his skin. If he knew what she had in mind then he wouldn't have thrown shorts on. He would've gladly stayed naked. But his angel surprised him. With his hands behind his head, he concentrated on the show unfolding in front of him. There was no doubt in his mind that he'd created a fucking monster. Cassandra enjoyed teasing him way too much.

The gentle sway of her hips caught his attention first and held it. The Country music she insisted on playing emanated throughout the room, those luscious hips keeping beat to the gentle roll of the guitar. Her hands floated over her body, slowly and with determination to caress every curve, every toned muscle.

Simply fucking amazing. That's what she was. Daren took a long steadying breath. At this rate, his cock would explode the moment she touched him.

"You like?" her voice teased.

Fuck yeah!

He couldn't risk talking for fear of begging, so he just nodded. His gaze continued to roam over her, taking in the mouth-watering sight. How a woman could look that sexy in a denim skirt and simple shirt was beyond him. But he didn't think the finest lingerie could compete right now. Not the way that denim clung to her hips, her belly button peaking out from the top. Her T-shirt molded to her breasts. His hands ached to take a hold of them, pinch those perky nipples until she cried out.

Her slim fingers worked her braid loose until she could dip her head and shake the massive mound of hair free. When she snapped her head back up, Daren drew a sharp, painful breath. God, she was stunning. The dark brown hair contrasted against her milky complexion; the allure of the waves of curly locks enough to draw a man to his knees for just a touch.

How he'd ever be able to walk away from her, he didn't know. When her fingers grabbed the hem of her T-shirt, he put that particular worry out of his mind for now. All he could focus on was the skin bared in front of him. He wanted her naked. He wanted her hot. He just fucking wanted her.

"Cassandra, baby. You're killing me. Rip those damn clothes off and get over here."

She smiled wickedly, and his gut tightened. Somehow he knew this wasn't a battle he'd win easily or any time soon.

"I'll take whatever punishment you'd like to dish out for my disobedience, but right now, Daren, I'm afraid you're going to have to sit and enjoy."

The little witch! Did she have any idea the challenge she just presented him? One look at the angelic face with the smile of the devil and he believed she knew exactly what she was doing to him. God, he loved her!

He what? What the hell? Where did that come from? He took a steadying breath and dismissed the notion. Of course he loved her. They were best friends. He adored her. Loved her as a friend, nothing more. Or did he?

His thoughts were interrupted when Cassandra freed her breasts from her bra. If he didn't pay attention to her striptease, he'd miss the whole damn thing.

"Take it all off, baby." Hell, he didn't care if he begged.

"In time."

A growl escaped his throat. If she didn't get naked soon, he'd help her.

His cock was hard as steel with its own heartbeat. His hand unzipped his shorts, offering minimal comfort to the engorged shaft. He dared to free it even with the fear of coming all over the bed as Cassandra danced. But if Cassandra wanted to tease him then he sure as hell would give it back. Her eyes widened as his hand gripped his cock, slowly moving up and down, his eyes never leaving her face. He loved the way her eyes brightened when she tried something new. By the way she was studying him, he'd bet she never witnessed a man masturbate before.

Watching her closely, Daren swallowed hard when she cupped her breasts, her thumbs flicking over the nipples until they stood erect and begged for his mouth. Her hands wandered over her belly to the top of her skirt and guided the material down over those luscious hips, smooth thighs, and toned legs. His cock bounced against his hand with every sway of her body. Since her panties had been removed earlier for the butt plug, she was now gloriously naked, standing in front of him.

"Come here, baby. I want to fuck you so bad."

There was that damn wicked smile again. "You can do that after your massage."

Oh hell no. He'd fuck her then she could massage him.

"Why don't you stand up and get naked for me now, Daren?"

No need to ask twice. He jumped from bed and stripped his T-shirt, shorts, and briefs off in seconds as she crawled onto the bed to watch.

"Wow. I got cheated. Where's the show? I gave you a nice one," she complained, her bottom lip turning into an adorable little pout that he wanted to nibble.

"Show's over, baby. Time to play."

He climbed onto the bed with visions of her slender body under his and his cock seated deep in her tight pussy. When she turned and jumped off the bed he was stunned.

"What the hell are you doing?" he asked, watching her circle the bed.

"I promised you a massage and that's what I'm going to do. Lay on your stomach."

"Like hell. Get back in this bed."

She crossed her arms. "I will. As soon as you roll over."

"Cassandra." Damn if he didn't want to throw her over his knee right now and paddle her ass until it glowed. Thoughts like that would make him come too soon, but her defiance was turning him on beyond his control.

"Daren."

He stared at her for a long moment. His Dominant

side wanted badly to teach her what such insolence got her. He'd have her tied to the bed in a flash, begging to be fucked, and keep her on the edge of orgasm until she trembled from just his breath on her skin.

But there was something in the gleam in her eyes. She wasn't trying to be difficult or purposely being disobedient. He saw submission. If he hadn't looked closely enough, he'd have missed it. He saw need, a need to please.

His heart somersaulted and pounded. Christ, she was giving him what he wanted, what he yearned for, and he was too damn blind to see it.

He caught hold of her arm before she could run away. Her eyes widened, shock covering her face. With controlled strength, he pulled her to the edge of the bed while he knelt on it. Lowering his head, he drank from her lips with a kiss intended to give her approval, encouragement, and support.

Ending the kiss, he did as she'd requested and lay on his stomach, naked and vulnerable. He knew he was the Dominant, but damn didn't she have all the power.

She quickly straddled his legs. The softness of her bare pussy lips passed over the back of his thighs as she moved onto him, stretching to touch his shoulders, smoothing on a slippery liquid over his skin.

"What's that?"

"Baby oil. Found it in the bathroom." Her voice, suddenly husky and full of need, crooned to his ears.

"I'd much rather be spreading it all over your naked body, baby," he told her, his head sideways on the pillow.

"And take away all of my fun?" She nipped at his ear lobe.

Christ, he may have agreed to this damn massage, but he didn't say it would be a long one. A few minutes. Tops. Then he had to have her.

Her hands began with a velvety caress of his muscles. Digging into the tissue, she manipulated each muscle, easing the tension. It was pure heaven the way her soft hands worked his hard skin. Relaxation swept over him even as his cock lay hard under his body. The supple curves of her ass slid up and down the back of his thighs as her hands splayed over his shoulders and back of his neck. The gentle scraping of her nails against his rigid skin sent fire straight to his groin, the sensation tightening his gut and electrifying every nerve ending in his body.

Breathing was nearly impossible with every breath taking in her lilac and vanilla scent. Closing his eyes, he envisioned laying her down in a bed of lilacs, the light purple petals smothering her skin with their fragrance. Lust stirred deep within his blood. He wouldn't be able to hold off fucking her much longer. His cock agreed, the throbbing head intent on burying itself within the walls of her pussy.

"Daren," she whispered into his ear.

He opened his eyes, but kept his head still. Her quiet voice was graced with an edginess that grabbed his attention and held it.

"Will you fuck me now?"

No other declaration would've shot him out of bed faster. With a growl, he twisted his body around, capturing her and flipping her from his legs with his sudden movement.

"I thought you'd never ask, baby," he told her, his own voice laced with his desire.

His mouth claimed hers, roughly, swiftly. Not able to get enough of the taste of her, his tongue plundered deep into the warmth of her mouth, swirling everywhere. There wasn't a nook or crevice within her he didn't touch, explore, devour.

Daren placed Cassandra under his body, her back on the bed and her lips still sealed with his. Leaning up on one arm to keep most of his weight off of her smaller frame, he moved his other hand frantically over her delicate skin. He needed to touch her everywhere. To feel her softness.

Breaking away from the kiss, he removed a condom from the nightstand, and quickly sheathed his cock. Returning to Cassandra, Daren smoothed his lips along her jaw, nipping his way to her throat. The beautiful skin along her neck was made for feasting. Sucking, licking, biting, it was all he could do not to swallow her up.

"Oh, Daren. Oh, yes. It feels so good."

"You taste even better," he acknowledged.

His head descended lower until his lips found her breast. When he took the nipple into his mouth, she shrieked as his teeth clamped gently over the hard peak. Sucking like he'd never get his fill of her, he alternated between breasts, wanting both in his mouth at once.

His arms trembled as he held his body off hers, but it wasn't from the weight. Working out and pumping iron gave him strong muscles, the simple act of holding himself up was barely a challenge. Controlling his passion made him shake like a goddamn teenager. He wanted Cassandra in every way possible.

Now all he wanted was to feel her soft muscles mold around him as he entered her pussy the way he'd dreamed of doing. With an intense determination, he flipped her onto her belly to change their position. His arm scooted under her hips to push her ass into the air as he held her arms behind her back. When she moaned, his cock flexed painfully. Without further delay, he positioned his cock at the entrance to her pussy.

Pushing the head through her soft muscles, he yelled out, "Fuck!"

Moving underneath him, Cassandra's supple body heated his flesh everywhere it touched. Fire would've been colder than what he was feeling.

With a long, determined thrust, his cock was finally where it begged to be, seated deep inside her quivering, warm cunt. Taking a moment to reign in his control, Daren hovered behind Cassandra, one arm stretched on one side of her and the other still securing her hands behind her back. Completely at his mercy, she moaned softly, threatening to undo the last of his composure.

Looking down was a mistake. The woman stole the last breath from his lungs, stole his very heart. Cassandra lay sprawled under him, her cheek resting on the mattress, eyes half closed, skin flushed where he had kissed her neck. He couldn't tear his eyes from her face. When her head turned and she looked back at him, his heart pounded so hard in his chest he was sure he'd go deaf from the sound.

"Daren?" her whispered question snapped him back to reality.

"You're gorgeous, baby. So pretty. So soft."

Her demure smile threatened to snap the last of his resolve. He moved his hips against her heat, wanting this moment to last forever.

His cock won the battle of wills though as his thrusts grew in depth and speed. She cried out, moaning in the most erotic way he'd ever heard.

"Come for me, baby. I want to feel you come so hard," he demanded. "You have permission."

He released her arms to reach between their bodies, brushing the junction of her legs. His fingers found their prize when they touched the hard nub of her passion. When he pinched her clit, she screamed out in pleasure. If not for his body weighing her down, he swore she would've shot off the bed.

"Daren! Daren! Daren!"

Over and over she screamed his name, the sound drowning out the Country song playing in the background. Nothing sounded more beautiful than her screaming his name in passion.

Her inner muscles clamped onto his cock, wave after wave of orgasm riding his shaft until he could hold back no more.

"Cassandra!" he said between gritted teeth as his cock erupted into the condom, wishing the barrier didn't exist and he could feel her hot pussy gliding over his cock. Each thrust carried more cum from his balls until he was sure there was none left. Against her pussy walls, his cock pulsed, the heat from her channel soothing the spent organ through the thin latex.

His cock fell free of her grip as he rolled off of her and she turned onto her back. Her beautiful brown eyes were dark with passion. He loved that look on her.

A fine coat of perspiration covered his skin and

hers. Looking at her, he knew at that moment he loved her. Not as a best friend. As a woman. He loved Cassandra and probably always had.

Now he had to figure out what the hell to do with that breakthrough.

"You look mystified, Daren. Was it not good?"

"More than good, baby." He kissed the tip of her nose, not trusting himself with her mouth for fear of arousing them both again. Not a bad idea, but he needed time to get his control back. "You give a great massage, by the way."

Smiling, he crawled off of her and sat at the edge of the bed to take care of the condom. When he was done, he lay back against the pillows and scooped her onto his chest. Kissing the top of her head, he just lay there enjoying the hum moving through his body.

He felt so alive. More alive than he ever had.

Cassandra's fingers toyed with the hairs on his chest. "So what's my punishment for disobeying you earlier?"

His smile came too easily for him to stop. He was grateful his face was hidden in her hair. "I'll forgive you this time."

She turned her head to look up at him. Was that disappointment in her eyes?

"Really? I'm forgiven. But I thought I broke the rules."

He placed his hand under her chin and pulled her lips to his. She was so soft and sweet. He simply couldn't get enough of her.

"You didn't really break the rules, baby. Not after I thought about it."

"I don't understand."

"You were aiming to please me and I was just too damn horny to realize you didn't intend to be disobedient. Once I stopped thinking with my cock, I was able to see your submissiveness. It made me very happy, Cass."

"It did? Cool. Very cool."

He laughed. "Yes. Very cool."

She settled back onto his chest, her slender body warm and curvy. "I think I'm getting a hang of this submissive thing after all."

"I do believe you are, baby. But I'll be able to tell more by the end of our weekend together."

"I could never give up control of my life, but in the bedroom I do like it."

He tightened his arms around her. "I don't want any woman to give up control of her life for me. That's not my thing. It's about the transfer of power. And it's always got to be consensual."

"You said you like a woman who can think for herself, form her own opinion and express it."

Someone like you. "Exactly. So, Cass, do you see how being a submissive in the bedroom allows you to escape from the every day pressures of being in charge?"

She was practically purring in his arms. Hot damn. "Oh, yes. I'm beginning to realize that. Just don't know why I never realized this about myself before."

That makes both of us. "You probably just suppressed it."

His hand captured hers playing in the mat of chest hair and pinned it to keep it still, her touch driving him wild.

"Then you came along," she said teasingly.

His free hand stroked her arm slowly up and down, enjoying every second touching her. "Yes, then I came along, baby. I let my genie out of her bottle I guess."

They laughed, enfolded in each other's arms. Talking about his sexual needs like it was an everyday conversation for them.

How he wished it could be.

Chapter Six

"Did you enjoy your shower, Daren?" Cassandra asked, sitting on the deck soaking up the late afternoon sun.

Even as she squinted with the bright rays, she could still make out his handsome face, the hard angles and planes, the solid jaw, bright eyes. She noticed he'd shaved, much to her disappointment. She happened to thoroughly enjoy the scrape of his stubble over her skin. Just thinking of how his mouth had roamed over her jaw and neck had her pussy clenching, wanting more of his cock.

Christ, he was turning her into a nymphomaniac.

"I did. Couldn't stop thinking of you, though. You should've joined me like I requested."

She immediately recognized that tone. Looking into his eyes, she focused on the dangerous glint. Well, hell, she'd earned a delicious punishment by refusing the shower and hadn't even realized it.

Her smile formed long and wide.

"I wouldn't be smiling if I were you, Cass. You're in a lot of trouble."

She stretched like a lazy cat, feeling every bit of a feline tease. "Mmmmm. Do tell."

The proof of her situation was evident in the bulge

in the front of his dress shorts. The cream colored material did nothing to hide the outline of his massive erection.

His face may have remained serious, but his eyes danced. "Remember? I give the orders. Not you."

Quickly she slid into her submissive role surprised at how easily she could. "Yes, of course."

"Stand up." His voice was firm, but his eyes gave away his lust.

She did as told and stood, feeling completely relaxed from her rest in the sun.

"Turn around and place your hands on the railing. Then lean over."

Before she turned to do as he asked, she noticed the butt plug and lube in his hand. Her belly did a little flip-flop. She'd wondered when they'd get around to anal sex. She wasn't ashamed at being curious. They only had two days after all, and time was ticking away.

At the railing, she nervously looked up and down the sand, hoping no one had ventured down this far onto Daren's private beach. Just like she did in the parking lot earlier, she grew damp with arousal at the thought of someone witnessing their actions. It was the combination of nervousness and courage that forced her to shed her inhibitions and try something new.

Gently bending her across the railing so only her elbows rested on it, Daren used his knee to nudge her legs apart. Her bare feet were on a shady part of the deck so they didn't feel the sting from the sun-drenched surface.

When he rolled her skirt up, exposing her nakedness, she gasped. She still wasn't used to exposing her body to her best friend. Everything over the past twenty-four hours had moved so fast, it was no wonder she needed to adjust to this newfound closeness with him.

Daren spoke firmly. "Just so you know, the butt plug is *not* to be viewed as a punishment. It's only a tool to prep you for my cock."

"I understand."

"However, the sensual torture before I fuck your ass will be your punishment, baby. Next time, remember to do as I request."

The teasing cadence of his words stirred her blood like a wild fire raging through her body. That he could make her so needy with just that voice was truly remarkable. Of course, being told how she'd be taken sexually was no less thrilling.

"You'll feel my lubed fingers first, baby. Relax for me."

She did as told, concentrating on his fingers pushing at the rim of her ass. She could do this, taking his exploration again of her darkest hole. She wanted it.

Slowly, he inserted his finger, his free hand holding her waist steady. The pressure wasn't as severe as the first time, but it was definitely noticeable. Her muscles stretched as he inched in. The burning of her flesh as it accepted his finger shouldn't have been exciting, but it was. Her pussy dampened with her juices as the soft breeze blew air over her exposed pussy lips, the wetness obvious.

"Good girl, keep relaxing."

"Whoa," she yelped when his finger slid all the way in, sheathed tightly by her fiery muscles. It'll stop burning soon, she told herself over and over again,

145

using the chant to calm her body.

When he began delicately fucking her ass with his finger, stroking the length of her butt hole and back in again, she groaned as the pain/pleasure threshold quickly became more pleasure. Amazed at how quickly her body adjusted to his invasion, she breathed out long and slow, entranced by his efforts.

"You have the sweetest ass, baby," he said, his free hand moving over her cheeks, squeezing and grabbing. "I can't wait to have my cock inside this tight hole. I wish you could feel what I do. The tightness, the heat, the grip."

She moaned, unable to form a complete thought. Her body was possessed by a need so great and her pussy throbbed for attention. His finger abandoned her ass, leaving her wanting to be filled. He didn't disappoint her long. His hand returned to her ass, but this time two fingers slithered down her butt crack to explore her anus.

"Oh. Oh wow," she exclaimed, pushing her bottom back toward him.

Without any words, Daren worked his fingers in and out of her ass, the channel accepting him and relaxing as the pleasure surpassed the pain. She closed her eyes and inhaled the warm, salty air. Just beyond the sand, small waves crash onto shore. Seagulls squawked as they flew overhead. What a glorious end to a summer day. It matched her mood.

Daren continued to give her ass his complete attention. When he removed his fingers, she wondered what was next and her belly did a flip-flop with anticipation.

"I'm going to insert the butt plug now, Cass.

Remember to relax. You'll bear down when I tell you. Understood?"

"Yes," she whispered, biting her bottom lip. She needed to relax, knowing it made insertion easier.

The cool tip of the plug pressed against her asshole, the tightness evident in the resistance the plastic met when pushed in gently.

"Oh," she cried out, but reminded herself to breathe. Relax and breathe. He'd take good care of her.

Daren slowly inserted the device, the lube running down her perineum to mix with her vaginal fluids. Her sex whimpered for his touch, but he kept to his task at hand.

Her inner muscles stretched, taking the plug deeper and deeper.

"Almost in, Cass. Bear down now."

With that statement, he turned the wider base past the resisting muscles as she bore down and seated the plug firmly in her ass.

"Oh!" she moaned, her breathing increasing. "Oh, that's tight, Daren."

His strong arms helped her stand up, turning her into his embrace. She clung to his T-shirt, her butt feeling full and tender.

"The hard part's over, Cass. Let your body accept it. Let it prepare your body for me, baby. I so want to have my cock in your ass tonight. It's all I've thought about all day."

"I'm trying. I feel like such a wimp."

He laughed and pulled her face against his chest and rubbed her back. "You're a virgin at this part of sex, baby. Remember, the first time's always the hardest." He pulled her face up to look into her eyes.

"If you trust me, I promise to make it very, very pleasurable for us both."

The plug was already feeling better, her ass not burning so much and the tightness was easing. "I do trust you. And I do want you to, well, fuck me there. It's just a little uncomfortable."

"You're doing great. But if you continue to be uncomfortable then I'll take it out and we'll wait for another time."

She looked at him in surprise. "As the Dom, aren't you suppose to make me take it no matter what?"

He frowned. "Hell no. You placed your trust in me to keep you safe in all of our sexual exploits. It's my responsibility to make damn sure you don't experience harm or any pain that's not directly related to pleasure."

She wiggled her butt to see if the discomfort was still there, but was pleased to feel it dissipating. "I could never do this with anyone else, Daren. I couldn't trust another man to take such good care of me."

His eyes darkened, the gleam dangerous and possessive. His mouth caught her by surprise when it crushed down on hers, his lips bruising hers in an intriguing kiss filled with heat and power. His hand gripped her hair, holding her to him. She was a captive in his embrace and loved it.

The kiss deepened until he stole her breath. She couldn't get enough of him. His strength held them both up as she leaned on him for support, her knees suddenly wobbly and her head dizzy. His taste was unique, a hot mint flavor born out of the passion he had for her mouth. Every stroke of his tongue against hers sent a jolt of awareness straight to her pussy.

Without thinking twice, her hands frantically unzipped his dress shorts and freed his hard cock.

He moaned against her lips. His hand tightened in her hair. Breaking the kiss, he pulled her head back and looked into her eyes. The wild gaze excited the raw animal passion in her.

Their hands took on a life of their own as they tore at their clothes, frantically removing any obstacle to their passion. Naked and standing in the fading sunlight on the deck, Cassandra sensed this was a different kind of lovemaking for them. This was a possession. They both claimed the other, if for just the moment.

When his hands suddenly stopped hers and held them tightly, she stared at him in shock.

"Not so fast, Cassandra. You're being punished remember?"

Her eyes widened. "You said the butt plug wasn't punishment though."

"It's not. But you don't get to come until I say."

"What?" she exclaimed, her pussy whimpering in protest.

"I want to hear you beg to come. And I plan to tease you so good that you won't forget this punishment."

"What?" Her voice quivered, not from fear but from helplessness. Her pleasure was totally in his hands and she was powerless to stop him. It excited her more than any other foreplay ever had as her pussy lips warmed with her juices. She swallowed hard and could only stare at him.

His eyes filled with lust. "You'll learn that when I make a request of you, I expect you to obey me."

Obey. The simple word held so much power. And stiffened her back. He expected her to *obey* him? Well, of course he did, she reminded herself. That's what he liked sexually, his partner to obey his commands for both their pleasure. And didn't she want to please him so much?

"Okay. I promise to from now on, Daren. But I need to feel you inside me now." She was unsuccessful in releasing his grip no matter how hard she struggled.

His stern look didn't frighten her but reinforced the fact that she was being punished. His terms. His way. Period.

Damn. If she didn't get this submissive rules stuff under control she'd die of needing to come. She had no doubt Daren was capable of holding her on the edge of orgasm until he desired her to have one.

"I'm sorry, Daren," she said humbly, her eyes cast down. "It won't happen again."

His cock flexed and she understood the power of her submission. She was captivating him with her submission. Never would she think she could compete with his strength, but right now she was so much more powerful and finally understood her role in his pleasure. She smiled at his cock, knowing she'd feel it soon, when Daren determined she deserved it. What an arousing thought.

"I hope not, Cass. I understand there's a learning curve here," he said, his hand moving under her chin to tilt her head up until her eyes met his. "But I expect you will make the best effort from now on not to test my patience."

She couldn't help it when a slight smile crept into the corners of her mouth. She hoped he didn't notice.

"I will. Promise."

His grin softened his serious expression. "Little devil. I saw that smile."

Her heart pounded. The last thing she needed was to piss him off so he held off her orgasm even longer.

"Relax." He kissed the corner of her mouth. "Lucky for you, I happen to enjoy when you look forward to your punishments."

When her smile erupted, she couldn't stop it. "I'm trying so hard, Daren. Really I am."

"I know, baby. But you did earn your punishment. So I must give it."

The look in his eyes thrilled her pussy. She could never be afraid of Daren even under the threat of a punishment. But her body welcomed his threats. Heated with his promises. Begged for his manipulations.

"Close your eyes and don't open them or I'll blindfold you."

She did as told. The loss of sight only increased her awareness of his hard body in her personal space. She relied on her other senses to monitor his movements and swore she could feel his shadow cover her skin, heating it when it should've cooled. His musky scent teased her nose telling her he stood very close.

His strong hands gently grasped her upper arms and helped her lean her butt against the railing. "Open your legs wide, Cass."

Feeling so vulnerable, she fought the urge to disobey. Slowly, she did as he commanded, feeling every bit exposed as she was meant to be.

"I love to taste your pussy, baby. I can see your

juices covering your pretty bare folds," he said, his warm breath tickling her inner thighs.

When his fingers caressed through the slick folds to her clit, she whimpered and trembled.

"I hope you're thinking of why you're being punished, baby. You should also be thinking of how you can avoid this in the future."

She bit her tongue against a sharp retort. The bastard! Of course she didn't want to avoid this ever.

His tongue swiped over her clit and ignited a firestorm through her blood. Her nails dug into the wood of the railing as she squeezed her eyes shut to be sure not to open them and prolong her punishment. He licked her folds slowly, flicking over the clit with each pass. His finger entered her pussy in a long teasing stroke.

He was devastating her thought process. Her mind was blank as the only focus of her attention was the pulsing needs gathering in her pussy. Her clit ached and begged for his touch. With every stroke of his finger, her pussy tightened.

She wouldn't survive this much longer. With her eyes closed, all she could envision was his thick cock filling her demanding cunt.

"So delicious, Cass. I could feast on you just like this…for hours."

She was defenseless to stop the cry that erupted from her lips. Hours? She wouldn't last a few minutes let alone hours. Begging was suddenly not beneath her.

"Please. Daren. Please."

His devilish tongue swept over her clit and she yelled out again.

"Please what?"

"Please make me come."

"Giving orders now, Cass? Looks like you have a long lesson ahead."

Her strangled cry cut the summer air like a knife. "No. Not giving orders. Just need to come."

"Beg."

Her orgasm hinged on a three-letter word. Jesus! How did she get herself into this? She was a fool to think she was a match for Daren's sexual appetite.

"Please!"

Did he just laugh? She'd kill him when she got her strength back.

"My dear, Cass. You can do much better than that. In fact, you have to."

Damn it! She willed her mind to focus on forming words as he continued his torturous manipulations of her aching pussy.

"I'm begging you, Daren. Please allow me to come." She took a deep breath and exhaled before continuing. "Please. I'm begging you. I need to come. I can't stand it. Please. Please. Let me come, Daren."

She didn't realize her hands had left the railing and were fisted in his hair holding his face to her pussy. Terrific! Now she'd never be allowed to come. Just when she was ready to beg for sweet mercy, that amazing mouth closed over her throbbing clit and sucked hard. The pull of his lips on her clit ignited her orgasm like a stick of dynamite. Her body sagged and trembled as each wave shot through her womb.

Daren stood, leaving her breathless against the railing.

"Daren? Can I open my eyes?"

"Yes, baby. I want you to watch me." His voice

153

was as strangled as hers had been a few minutes ago. One look at his face and she noticed holding off her orgasm hadn't been easy on him either. Tension radiated from his body.

Her pussy lips were still spasming while her eyes adjusted to the sunlight.

He quickly unwrapped a condom and expertly sheathed his massive erection. With two long steps he was back in front of her, his cock flexing against her belly. He lifted her and pulled her legs around his waist, pressing her back against the railing as she locked her hands behind his neck. With an urgency she'd never felt before, Daren entered her soaked pussy, the intrusion reminding her that she still wore the butt plug as the pressure from her cunt created sensations in her ass. What she noticed first was the fullness, both holes pulsing with their own needs, their own aches. The feeling was dazzling, exhilarating, to be taken in such an erotic way. She wanted to share herself in every way with Daren, needed him to teach her what it was he wanted from her.

Could she satisfy him like this forever or would he get bored? But forever didn't exist for them. The reality of their weekend arrangement hit her in the gut like a sucker punch. She'd worry about that later. She just wanted Daren.

"Cassandra, you feel amazing."

When his hand moved around her ass and touched the butt plug, strong vibrations penetrated her virgin channel.

"What the…oh God, that feels so good."

"Did you forget about the vibrator?"

Whoever invented that was her hero. The light

humming helped ease her muscles, allowing her to feel more of the plug's presence, to feel more bliss.

His hips flexed into her sweet spot, the rhythm fast but steady. When he continued to fuck her steadily with long, determined strokes that reached all the way to her womb, she felt like the surf in the distance behind her. Her body rolled over and over inside with waves of pleasure that increased with each movement of his hips. As ocean swells pounded onto the shore, waves of ecstasy crashed through her pussy. Slowly, the tug of another orgasm built. Closing her eyes, she gave her body over to the excitement spiraling through her.

"Oh, yes. Daren. Oh my God. Please let me come." It surprised her how asking for permission to come was almost automatic.

"Come, baby. Come."

His lips crushed to hers, claiming her mouth with a kiss that reached her very soul. The emotion vibrating from him was contagious. She kissed him suddenly unable to get enough of him, unable to get close enough. She wanted more. Oh God, how she wanted more of this man she loved. She choked on a sob as the intensity of their loving claimed her heart, branding his name on it forever. No matter what happened after they returned home, she'd always remember these hours of passion spent in his arms.

Her pussy contracted violently, the lips pulsating around his thick cock, drawing him into her hot core, and soaking him with her juices. The orgasm roared through her body, his cock lighting fires every place it stroked deep within her.

Unable to breathe, she broke the kiss. A wildness

enveloped her, revealing a woman who only lived for the moment, only existed for this ride with Daren. Her hips bucked wildly against his, hardly aware of her ass cheeks hitting against the railing. The butt plug remained secured in her anus with the vibration level at its highest, adding to the glorious sensations riveting through her body.

She trembled, leaned into his shoulder, and sank her teeth into the hard muscles. He moaned and pounded his cock deeper, stilling once his cock found release. His hips thrust and held, thrust and held, like he never wanted to stop. Her hands roamed through his thick hair now damp with sweat. Her mouth rested against the side of his neck, his pulse jumping under her lips.

His strength held up her sagging body, keeping her locked safely in his arms until their passion was spent and their orgasms subsided. Slowly, he eased her to her feet to stand in front of him.

Breathless, Daren pulled his erection from her soaked pussy and removed the condom. He picked up their discarded clothes, scooped her into his arms, and walked into the house without saying a word. She held on tightly, her arms linked around his neck. Her body felt like an electrical wire dancing in the street during a storm. She was far from being sated.

Daren entered his bedroom and placed her in the middle of the king-sized covered bed.

"Don't move," he warned, left the room, and returned in less than a minute with the bag from the sex toy store.

Her body tingled as he moved about the room. His naked ass was a gorgeous sight. It was firm and muscular. Her hands itched to run over it.

From a nightstand by the bed, he removed a set of restraints and sent her a mischievous look when he attached them to the bedposts at the headboard.

"I wonder if you're ready for the next step in pleasing my Dominant side," he said, his voice rough and eager.

Her belly flipped in anticipation, her nervousness a natural reaction that heightened her arousal. She reminded herself that she'd asked him for this; it was one of her fantasies to be tied up.

"Of course. I want to learn all that I can from you, Daren."

She didn't miss the flash of lust in his eyes. She noticed that when she encouraged his teachings and instructions, the intensity in his eyes changed instantly to excitement and desire.

When his strong hand clamped over her wrist pulling her arm above her head to the first restraint, panic set in. She resisted, trying to pull her arm back to her body. She wanted this, but now that it was happening, it was a little intimidating. To not be able to move, to be held in place was a frightening aspect. She didn't know if she could do this.

"Maybe this part should just remain a part of my fantasy, Daren."

He stopped and leaned down to kiss her lips gently, before meeting her eyes with a thoughtful stare. "Don't be afraid. I'd never hurt you. Just give yourself a chance to try this. If you don't like it, baby, all you have to say is stop and I will release you. Okay?"

She bit her bottom lip, but nodded for him to continue. When both her hands were secured above her and she lay naked and vulnerable, he stepped back, moving his gaze up and down her body, devouring her like she was a last meal. She couldn't help but squirm, testing the strength of the restraints and realizing she was firmly locked in place. Her heartbeat sped up, this was the most arousing act she'd ever participated in even more so than the butt plug still humming in her ass.

Daren moved over her body, his lips sucking her nipple, his palm squeezing her breast. His teeth bit gently onto the pink nipple, sending a line of fire straight to her groin. Her pussy clenched as she writhed under the weight of his body, trying desperately to rub her clit against his cock with no luck.

"No, Cass. You have no control in this now. I'll pleasure you as I see fit."

Her eyes widened and stared up at him, his face inches from hers. "That's *so* not fair. Fuck me now, Daren. I want to have you inside me. Please."

"No. Not before I taste you again. Consider this part of your punishment as well. You'll come when I'm ready to allow it."

His words awakened her pussy once again, the juices flowing over her lips to be teased by the air around them.

He ignored her whimpers, and yes, she did whimper, using every means to get what she wanted— his cock buried deep inside her. After the earlier loving and those tremendous orgasms, Cass had no right to need him again so soon. But he made her insatiable.

When he trailed wet kisses down her belly to her inner thighs, she thought she'd die if he didn't fuck her madly. But as his demanding mouth settled onto her pussy lips and licked her silken folds slowly up and down, she knew she'd died and gone to heaven. Nothing in her life had ever felt so damn good. Even though her body still hummed from her earlier orgasms, this was like having a never-ending orgasm. Every stroke of his tongue heated her flesh, charged her muscles, swelled her labia. The ache began in her throbbing pussy lips, slow and steady like the hum of a small motor, then grew with each pass of his tongue as he licked over her folds in long, soft caresses. The throbbing soared through her womb to places deep inside her that begged for his cock. The vibrations from the butt plug teased her ass reminding her what would soon replace it—Daren's hard cock. Excitement threatened to overwhelm her.

His thumbs spread her pussy open. The touch of his rough fingertips over her soft skin heightened her arousal. Her body was no longer hers, it belonged to him, begging and pleading for the heat from his mouth.

Pulling against the bindings got her nowhere, just reminded her of her predicament. Daren was punishing her deliciously, for reasons she couldn't remember and didn't care, although she'd love to break that rule again if it meant this kind of treatment.

Cassandra's hips arched to meet his kisses, his tongue darted in and out of her wet hole, fucking her solidly until she was on the verge of exploding, only to stop, leaving her hanging on for dear life. Her fingers flexed open then closed, her arms still held firmly by the restraints. This was killing her. She needed to come.

"Daren! I need to come. I can't take this."

His mouth pulled away from her pussy lips. He looked up at her over her belly, his lips wet with her juices. The scent of her arousal filled the air, a musky fragrance of her sex weeping.

"The next time you'll obey my rules, Cass. Won't you?"

The stern look he shot her before burying his mouth back between her legs was filled with promise. He was enjoying this as much as she was drowning in the pleasure. The bastard! Payback would be swift once she got his cock into her mouth. She'd show him what it was like to have your whole body lit up like a firecracker that never got to explode. Maybe she had a touch of Dominant in her.

Her thoughts of revenge were quickly replaced with desperate need as his mouth continued the same delicious tactics on her pussy. That amazing tongue fucked her pussy hole, while his finger twirled hard circles around her clit.

"Oh, hell. This is too much to handle. I can't."

He ignored her, of course, and continued licking her pussy like he was a starved man. The soft slurping sounds coming from between her legs drove her closer to the edge, where she dangled precariously, waiting for the power of the orgasm to overtake her.

"You taste so sweet, Cass."

Daren's fingers caressed her wet flesh, her pussy lips quaking.

"Daren!" She stared down at him again, pulling against the binds and rattling the headboard.

His lips grew into a dazzling smile, but she was in no mood for that now. "You'll obey me always, now won't you, baby?"

"Yes!"

"You may ask for permission to come."

What? She had to fucking ask again? Oh, this submission business was so hard to learn.

"You must ask me, Cassandra," he said when she didn't speak. His voice was low, like he could wait all day, his finger continuing to stroke the wet, swollen folds of her pussy.

Her blood roared through her ears and she could barely hear him. But her body needed release.

"May I come, Daren?" she asked, her words breathy and strained.

His hesitation made her nervous. There was no way she could take any more of this punishment no matter how delicious he made it.

"Yes, my dear. You may."

With that, he bent his head and his mouth covered the small bud of her clit and sucked it hard. Damn. He was an expert at this. Her hips arched to meet his kiss. If it weren't for the restraints holding her back, she would've grabbed hold of his head to keep him in place.

Bright flashes of light blinded her as a wave of unimaginable bliss swept over her, catapulting her to a place high in the heavens and keeping her there as his mouth worked relentlessly, licking and sucking her pussy and clit. Her hands continued to fight against the binds that held her helplessly in place. She wanted to reach for him, to taste him as he was her, giving him pleasure in return.

Daren moved over her body with the finesse of a tiger on the prowl. The dark penetrating stare of his brown eyes mesmerized her from where she lay helplessly in her binds as he came to a stop when his hips were over hers.

He allowed her no time to recover before he plunged his cock into her pussy, burying it as deep as it would go. She never even saw him put the condom on, but when he slipped into her wetness she felt the heat of his erection through the thin latex sheath.

He fucked her with a desperation born of hunger, and she couldn't get enough of him. Every climax left her wanting more. His thick cock filled her mercilessly, seeking its own comfort, but rewarding her when it hit her G-spot. The thick head rammed into her G-spot sending shock waves throughout her womb. The ripple effect went on forever. She writhed under his body, not trying to escape, but trying to move him faster. She needed his cock to fuck her harder, faster, deeper, arching her hips to make it happen.

"Cass, baby. You have no idea how great you feel. So tight. So hot." His voice was strangled by the raw need.

Oh, she definitely had a clue about how good their loving felt. It transformed her body from strong bones to a pile of ash, desire dueling with the need to release. It was a fine line to hover and she was barely holding on. She didn't want to lose the glorious tremors filling her cunt, but needed to feel the explosion they promised.

With his hips slamming into hers and his rigid arms holding his weight off her, his eyes caught hers and held. She was mesmerized by the desire flickering in the brown depths, his focus only on her.

She swore his cock swelled inside her as it crammed against her vaginal walls, stealing her breath with each thrust. His pubic bone teased fiery sparks from her clit. If only she could touch herself, she would come instantly.

"Oh. Daren. I need…to come. I'm right there."

"Cassandra." His voice held warning.

Unable to resist the urge to beg, she spoke loudly. "Daren, please may I come?"

"Yes."

He sucked in air, a low growl emanating from his throat to thrill her even more. Her submission fueled his fires, giving him what he needed to satisfy his desires. She witnessed it as every angle and plane on his handsome face hardened with the tension strumming through his body as he fucked her like a man on a mission–determined. His body against hers, she could feel the heat emanating from him, could feel the humming of his entire body as he rammed his cock deep into her. Her pussy was ever so grateful for the attention as it released more of its juices to slide over his erection.

Fucking her wildly, their bodies glistened with sweat, his head flung back, as he finally held himself deep inside her, sending his release toward her womb only to be captured by the condom. The restriction on her movement reminded her she was still restrained and at his mercy. She screamed out, wanting to grab onto him. Sensing her need, he collapsed onto her, his strong arms wrapping around and sliding under her back to hug her fiercely, protectively. Her womb continued to convulse, the orgasm sending its shock waves throughout her pussy.

After a moment, he leaned up and looked down. "You okay?"

She was breathless. "More than okay. I just wish I could touch you or hold you."

He smiled. "Nice try, baby. But I still have plans for you. You're not getting out of these just yet. Remember, I'm in control."

He nibbled at her shoulder, trailing kisses over the sensitive curve of her neck. His erection had softened but remained impressive and rubbed against her belly as he tortured her with sweet kisses.

Slowly, he shoved off of her to lie by her side. "I just need a few minutes, baby. You're giving my cock the best workout its ever had."

"Then I should be rewarded."

He smiled. "How so?"

"A cool drink would be nice."

"Anything for you. Be right back."

Cassandra looked around the room in awe. If she were dreaming, she prayed she wouldn't wake up any time soon.

Daren quickly returned with a tall glass of iced tea. When he held it to her lips, she drank deeply, reminded that she was bound.

He lay beside her after placing the glass on his nightstand. "You're amazing, Cassandra."

"Really?"

"Absolutely. You're driving me wild. I don't think I'll ever get rid of my hard-on when you're around."

She laughed, enjoying the compliment. "And here I thought I was making everything too difficult with my screw-ups."

"Baby, you're perfect. You challenge me in so many ways that I crave. You don't screw up. You make sex very interesting."

She smiled shyly. "Wow. I thought you'd be upset that I couldn't be a good submissive right away."

He shook his head. "Nonsense. It's not a job, Cass. It's part of you. You still have inhibitions about accepting your submissive side. That won't change overnight, but you're making remarkable progress."

"Really?"

"Yes, baby. I've enjoyed every minute with you. And guess what?"

"What?"

"I'm ready for you again."

He wasn't lying, she noticed as she glanced at his cock jutting out at full mast.

She couldn't help but purr.

His hand slid under her bottom and grasped the butt plug tugging gently. "Relax, baby. This is coming out."

The first thing she noticed was the vibrations that had soothed her stretched virgin ass had ceased. As the plug was pulled from her body, she relaxed but the burning sensation in the wake of its removal caused her to gasp. And then finally, it came free.

"I'm going to fuck your ass like I've dreamed of doing."

Her body reacted instantly, her pussy clenched, her breath hitched, and her ass tingled. God, yes, this is what she'd fantasized about for so long.

Kneeling on the bed, he opened the nightstand drawer to retrieve a bottle of lube.

When he released her wrists from the restraints, she was confused.

"Onto your belly, baby. It'll be easier for me to get to that sweet ass," he said, offering his hand for assistance.

She did as he said and quickly rolled over. His hands were there instantly to refasten the bindings. She felt even more vulnerable in this position. But she had to put her trust in Daren. He'd never harm her. Her pussy agreed as it ignited with a heat so intense she expected to set the bed on fire.

"This is just my finger with some lube."

It slid into her anus amazingly easy, the soft stroking of his finger had her pussy clenching hard. Taking his time, his lubed finger slowly inched in and out of her anal opening. There was no burning, just a teasing caress.

But just the thought of his thick cock entering her ass was enough to make her wonder if she could actually handle such an invasion. She bit down on her lip and squeezed her eyes shut.

"Don't tense up, Cass. You need to relax. I'll take good care of you. I promise."

She knew he would, but the fear of the unknown was both scary and exciting all at once. That long finger probed her darkest channel, moving in and out slowly, caressing her erotically. The tingling sensation it left in its path was like a jumpstart for her pussy. The lips swelled and her juices flowed freely down her thighs with her growing arousal.

Closing her eyes again, she gave herself over to the sexual tension riveting through her body, every nerve cell on high alert. The anticipation was building to a torturous level.

When he removed his finger, she whimpered, enjoying his touch so much. But her disappointment was short lived when he entered her again, this time with two fingers. The added digit widened her flesh more, stinging a little, but the awareness escalated her arousal.

Daren bent to kiss her cheek, before speaking in a controlled manner, his desire apparent as he looked at her like she was the only woman he'd ever seen. "I need to make sure I prepare you really well since my cock is a lot thicker than my fingers or the butt plug."

Just hearing him admit that sent her system into overload, every part of her body was aware of his intentions. Her belly tightened into knots. "Daren, I'm nervous it'll hurt. But I do want this. I want you to fuck me in my ass."

His voice was soothing. "Just think of the pleasure I'll show you."

She writhed under his touch, the binds holding her securely. She wanted to touch him, touch herself.

His fingers continued their journey, stroking the length of her asshole, each pass loosening her more, her muscles easing to allow smooth movement.

"This little ass of yours is so hot," he declared, his voice strangled. "I love the feel of your tight ass wrapped around my fingers. Do you know I can feel you quiver with every stroke?"

Could he really be torturing himself as much as he was her with this foreplay and preparation? Good. Serves him right to have his body so charged and waiting for the moment they were joined and racing to their relief.

Cassandra moaned, the probing getting faster. "It's so tight. I don't think your cock will fit. You're too big."

"I won't have a problem, baby. It's time to find

out."

"Oh God."

He leaned down to her face, his nose almost touching hers. "I need to ask you, Cass. I want to go bareback. I've always used a condom before, so I'm clean. No worries."

She knew better than to worry with him. "Okay."

"So you wouldn't mind if I skipped the condom now?"

She shook her head. "Not at all. I was hoping you would. Would rather feel you than latex."

"Oh hell yeah," he said before laying a noisy kiss on her cheek and standing back beside the bed.

She glanced over her shoulder just as his large hand smoothed the clear lube over his cock, making its length gleam.

"I want to feel your ass as I slip inside. I don't want to miss anything."

She inhaled sharply as his hand stroked that hard cock and she pictured what it would look like sliding into her ass. Glancing up at his face, she could see his barely controlled passion, his jaw tight and his eyes dark.

The bed dipped when he crawled back on. One hand lifted her ass in the air so that she had to kneel, using her elbows for support. Carefully, he positioned his lubed cock at the puckered entrance of her ass. He was so huge, she expected it to hurt like hell. Okay, she just had to trust him to know her limits. He'd take good care of her.

Her body tensed, her arms fought against the restraints until she reminded herself this was what she'd always wanted. She slowly relaxed as best she could.

"Cassandra." His tone warned since she wasn't being as submissive as he'd like.

When his thighs brushed against the back of hers, the moment was at hand. Daren was about to fulfill her anal sex fantasy. The mix of fright and lust combined to wind up the tension in her body, every touch of his body against her blazing.

Gently, he positioned his cock against the tight muscles of her anal opening. She gasped as he slid slowly into her, a pinch of pain combined with the thrill of a new adventure. Biting down on her bottom lip, she concentrated on breathing, slow and easy, relaxing her entire body.

His intrusion into this untouched part of her body provided new sensations she'd never guessed existed. The pleasure overwhelmed her as her anal muscles stretched to take him deeper. The slow burn crept through her ass to intensify the fire in her pussy.

"Oh God! You feel so good, baby."

"It hurts a little but I like it." She controlled her breathing as much as possible. It was so intense to feel his cock strumming against the tight muscles of her ass as he worked his way inside. Every thrust turned her on more, made her want to have him seated deep inside her already.

His intrusion stopped and she felt her body adjust and loosen.

"Let me do all the work, Cass," he said, his hand soothing over her back, rubbing small circles near her tailbone.

After a moment, his hips propelled into her backside again. The stretching increased as he inched in. She moaned loudly, her words inaudible even to her.

Her body slowly stretched to accommodate him, the burn bordering on the pain/pleasure line enhancing her desire to be taken faster. With each thrust, he hesitated a moment allowing her to get used to his size before he continued further. She pulled against the binds, their hold only increasing her arousal. The reality of not having her freedom proved she had to rely on Daren for her pleasure, comfort, and enjoyment. Would he really be that in tune to her body to deliver the ultimate satisfaction?

"Almost in, baby. Fuck this feels too good."

With one final flex of his hips, he was fully seated in her ass, the burning pulsed throughout her entire channel as her body slowly accommodated his size. She imagined how erotic the sight of his cock fucking her ass was and felt her pussy throb, the hint of orgasm just over the horizon.

The fullness consumed her. His position behind her provided a depth that reached to her soul. He'd obviously used a generous amount of lube because she could feel the excess sliding down to her wet pussy lips.

"How you doing, Cass, honey? It should be getting more comfortable."

"It is. Feels better than I imagined."

"Good. We'll take our time. Remember, if you ever want to stop just say 'stop.'"

"Okay. I don't want to stop, Daren. Please. I like it."

He shuddered, then moved slowly, pulling out a little then inching all the way back in. After a few minutes, the burn was replaced by a fullness she'd never expected would make her so horny.

"God, Cass, you are so tight. Hell yeah. Tell me if I go too fast. I'm trying not to lose control here."

"Daren," she gasped, struggling against her binds.

He stilled. "Yeah, baby. You okay?"

She was better than okay, she was out of her mind with need. "Fuck me. I want you to fuck my ass like you do my pussy. Fast. Hard."

He inhaled sharply as the heat from his body scorched hers. "Oh, Cass, baby. You have no idea what you do to me."

When his cock pulled back, she was afraid he'd fall out of her. She cringed, fearing he wouldn't get back inside since it was so tight. Relief flooded her when the thickness of his cock buried deep inside her ass again, grazing tender muscles, eliciting a moan from her lips.

His simple strokes in and out were slow and controlled, even when his thighs trembled against hers. His hand held her hips, those strong fingers dug into her skin offering another form of restraint as he easily held her in place.

The pressure built within her ass as his cock fucked her, carefully claiming her virgin hole. She moaned louder, unable to contain her approval of his fucking.

The feeling of having her ass fucked was better than she'd ever dreamed or could've imagined. This intimate act she'd feared would result in only pain was beyond erotic, allowing her to experience a part of her body she'd never had before. Maybe it was because of Daren's careful preparation that her body hummed like a thousand fingers on it. Or maybe it was because giving herself this way to the man she loved was the most intimate act she'd ever done. The sheer intensity dampened her eyes as a blissful feeling enveloped her. Whatever it was, it didn't matter.

Her body heated from deep within her ass, the slow spread of warmth moving through her belly, her womb, to her pussy and converging with a throbbing that propelled her body into a spiral of aches, pulses, and delicious spasms.

"Daren!" she screamed and exploded with the force of a mortar shooting from its cannon, her juices gushing from her throbbing pussy. The binds held her in place even as she writhed under the weight of his hips jamming into hers, her hips backing up to meet his, refusing to release him.

"Daren! Oh this...oh I can't...don't stop!"

With a loud groan, his body stilled as he emptied his seed deep into her ass. "Fuck yeah," he yelled, his deep voice booming throughout the room.

His hips were glued to hers and his hands grasped her waist as his thick cock filled her completely. The sensation of his cock crammed into her ass continued to strum her pussy with little pulses, each one making her gasp and never letting her forget how overly sensitive her cunt was right now. Her pussy walls were like a violin and his cock was playing a slow waltz on it.

Gasping for air, Cassandra allowed her elbows to take her weight as her hands remained tied to the headboard. The long tether did not give her much room to move. Her ass remained at the mercy of Daren's cock until his erection softened.

He pulled out of her slowly, the removal of his thickness creating a void that her body immediately protested. Her swelled pussy lips still quivered, tiny pulses running the length of her opening. If only she could touch herself, she'd be able to soothe the heated flesh.

Daren climbed off of her and quickly removed the restraints, massaging her wrists, before leaving her lying stretched out on her belly in the middle of the bed.

She was finally catching her breath when he returned from the bedroom and crawled back onto the bed to sit between her legs. Curious, she leaned up on her elbows and turned her head to look over her shoulder. She wouldn't have guessed what he was about to do, but it felt so damn good when he applied a warm wet washcloth to her ass and gently cleaned her.

The soothing touch swelled her heart. If she hadn't already been in love with him, she would've fallen head over heels at that moment for the tender attention he provided her. He crawled up the bed to lie beside her, his strong arms pulling her into a tight embrace, while he kissed the top of her head.

"That was amazing, Cass. Better than I ever dreamed. You're so beautiful."

"You fulfilled another of my fantasies." She looked up at him from her position on his chest. "I am still amazed you fit inside me."

"You were so tight. Just thinking about it is getting me hard again." He kissed the top of her head again, taking a deep breath from her hair.

Her body was so relaxed she could fall asleep. "I'd like to do it again soon, but it's a little tender. It felt so good though."

He laughed. "I'd love to do that again, but unfortunately I don't think your body would be up to it for some time. And we only have this weekend."

Reality came crashing down on Cassandra as she took in Daren's words. The reminder that their time together was limited was a direct blow to her heart. She hadn't wanted to think about it. To worry about what it would feel like once the weekend was over was too much to bear. Staring straight ahead at the empty wall, she swallowed hard and ushered the miserable thoughts from her mind.

"I have other plans for you." He said, moving her head back to look into her eyes.

"Do they happen to include food because I'm famished? I've worked up a bit of an appetite."

"Absolutely. First a shower."

Chapter Seven

Of course they couldn't just take a shower. No. Daren had to fuck Cassandra until she didn't know her name and her pussy sang with another mind-wrenching orgasm. How she ever lived without these orgasms, she didn't know. Worse, how was she ever going to live without them once Daren moved away? That was something to dwell on another time. Right now the spaghetti dinner Daren cooked was delicious and she was starving.

They sat on the deck, the sunset of orange and red lightened the evening sky. A warm breeze swept off the ocean, warning of a humid night ahead. The smell of salty air and wet sand set the mood even better than a violinist would have.

"You can always come work for me, Cass, and get out of that job you hate so much," Daren said, between bites of pasta.

Holding her fork mid-way to her mouth, Cassandra just stared at him. If only it was that simple. "That wouldn't be a good idea, Daren, and you know it."

"Why the hell not? I'll need a good accountant. Salary will beat what you make now. Hughes Ice Cream pays its employees above market value. We happen to be one of those rare companies that appreciates our staff."

The offer was so tempting. She'd been hoping to land another job, but there weren't many opportunities for accountants in the current market. She hated the thought of starting over somewhere, the loss of vacation time, seniority, and familiarity. Change made her nervous. Maybe that's why she always panicked when a guy got too close and wanted something more permanent than great sex and a dinner companion.

And then of course there were her parents to consider since she was their main caregiver thanks to her sisters always manipulating her time by having excuses not to run the errands for the folks. It would be nice to move away just to have a break from being the family errand girl.

"Agreed. Your company does have a great reputation for treating its employees well. But moving two states away is a lot to do. And now we've slept together."

He laughed. "All the more reason to move with me. It'll be hard for us to fuck with you in one state and me in another. And I'd love to fuck you more than just this weekend."

There it was again. His reminder that this weekend was just about the sex.

"So you want to extend the friends-with-benefits gig to more than just this weekend, huh?" she asked, trying her best to keep her voice normal.

He smiled wide. "Hell yeah. We're great in bed. And your submissive side is showing much improvement. Might as well let me continue to nurture it."

"What, until I get bored like I usually do with men?"

"Sure." His eyes darkened and his jaw set in that stubborn way when something crawled up his ass.

If he didn't like her casual response to his proposition—too bad. He'd never see her as anything more than a fuck buddy. What happened when that thrill wore off, like she knew damn well it would? Then she'd be stuck working for her ex-lover in a new state without her family near. It was too much to sacrifice when she already knew what the outcome would be...her heart broken.

"We can't work together, Daren. I've never slept with my boss before and it's not good to mix business with pleasure."

"Don't see why the hell not when we have great sex."

"Sex isn't everything, no matter how great it is. It's not acceptable to sleep with your employees, Daren."

"Sure it is if that employee was my wife."

She stared at him. "What did you say?"

His smile was devastating. "I guess that wasn't a classy marriage proposal. But I think I was clear enough. I love you, Cass. Marry me. We can build the New Hampshire business, start a life together."

Marry him? She couldn't have heard right.

"Did you just ask me to marry you?"

"I did. Now comes the part where you say you will."

Shock ran through her body. He wasn't the settling down type. How dare he tease her with a proposal when they both knew he'd change his mind

177

once he grew bored with her? Hell, they'd never even make it to the altar before he decided he'd only asked just to keep the great sex going. He hadn't even taken into consideration everything else that would get screwed up if they got married.

"Daren, you're asking too much of me. I'm sorry, but I can't marry you. It's not what you really want anyway."

His jaw tightened, his eyes narrowed. "Since when do you know what the hell it is I really want? I'm pretty sure this is exactly what I want since I've never asked another woman to marry me, and I sure the hell haven't declared my love for anyone else."

Her heart pounded so hard he'd surely see it through her chest. "Think about it, Daren. You don't really want to marry me. You're just enjoying the sex and, yes, it's been great. But that's no reason for us to tie the knot or for me to uproot my life and move two states away from everything I've ever known."

"You're wrong, Cassandra. I happen to think we're a match in every way."

She drank some wine for her dry throat. "If we didn't work out, I don't know if I could live without you as part of my life. I suck at relationships. You said it yourself. I discard men like a bad habit."

"Don't group me with all the other guys in your past, Cassandra. Don't tell me that what we've shared isn't special, more than special. We've discovered a once-in-a-lifetime love and I'm not letting you give it up because you dislike change."

"I'm afraid, Daren."

His eyes widened. "Of me?"

"Don't be ridiculous," she scolded. "I could never

be afraid of you. I'm just, well, this is all happening too fast. It still feels like a dream."

"I know you love me, Cass, baby. I can see it in the way you look at me, feel it in your touch."

"Of course I love you. You're my best friend."

His hand slammed on the table. "Damn it. It's more than that and you know it. You just won't admit it because then you'll have no excuse not to marry me."

She couldn't admit it. As much as she wanted to declare her love to him, she just couldn't. Her heart needed protection from the heartbreak that was sure to come when he realized he'd made a huge mistake. He'd probably laugh about it by morning while she slowly died inside.

Best friends. Fuck buddies. Friends-with-benefits. That's all they were. All they could ever be. Cassandra had to face reality for both of them.

"My answer is no, Daren. I won't marry you."

"Cassandra."

She shook her head to ward off his scrutiny. "I guess I didn't want to admit that having you as my lover could jeopardize our friendship. If it didn't work out, I don't know if I could live without you."

His hand covered hers. "It's a little too late for that since we're lovers now. But I'll give you time for this to sink in. But make no mistake, I won't sit at home in New Hampshire while you fuck other men. I won't share you, Cassandra. I don't desire any other woman but you. For now, I'll give you some time. And, of course, I still intend to use this weekend to convince you how good we are together."

****

Daren and Cassandra cleared their dishes from the deck, the evening air turning cooler with the hint of humidity. What he wouldn't give to spend every night like this, with Cassandra by his side, in his bed, with him.

He poured two glasses of wine, handed her one, then took her hand and led her into the large family room. The awkwardness of their earlier conversation still hung in the air, but he refused to waste one minute of their weekend arguing about why they were right for each other. Convincing her to move with him wouldn't be an easy job, but he had at least hoped asking her to marry him would show her, prove to her, that he was willing to make a commitment. She didn't have to fear commitment with him. He wanted to spend the rest of his life with her. There was no question in his mind or heart about that.

Maybe all these years it hadn't been the women's fault for not returning to his bed. Maybe he didn't make them feel desired enough to want to return. He'd always fantasized about Cassandra being the woman in his bed. And there was that one time he'd yelled Cassandra's name out while fucking that gorgeous black-haired actress. What the hell was her name? It escaped him and, truth be told, he couldn't even remember what her face looked like. He just remembered that her hair and body resembled Cassandra's. And, of course, he remembered her reaction to being called another woman's name. His cheek could still feel the sting of that slap.

Daren left Cassandra on the couch while he lit a

fire in the stone hearth, the focal point in the large family room. There were only two logs in it so the heat would be minimal. He wanted the night to be perfect so he could romance her, show her how their lives could be together. The surface of her kinkier side had only just been skimmed. Tonight, he planned to pull out all stops and deliver her the most intense orgasms, so memorable they'd be the only thing she would think of when away from him. Then she'd yearn for him, crave to be in his arms. He needed her to crave his companionship like he did hers. And maybe, just maybe, she'd stop being so damn stubborn and admit she was in love with him.

He glanced over at her sitting cozily on the couch sipping her wine, and knew he couldn't be wrong about that. He believed with every fiber of his being that Cassandra loved him more than just as a friend. If she didn't his heart would never recover. He could never feel for another woman what he felt for Cassandra. She had to know there was nothing he wouldn't do for her.

He walked to the couch and picked up his wine glass and sat next to her.

"A toast," he said, raising his glass. "To the most wonderful woman a man can call his friend and be fortunate enough to have feasted on her beauty."

The clink of the glasses echoed in the room as she stared at him. When her lips touched the rim and drank slowly, he swallowed hard, wishing it was his cock she had those pretty pink lips around and was drinking his cum. He took a long swallow of the merlot before placing the glass back on the coffee table.

His hand wrapped around her bare ankle and

pulled it onto his lap and then did the same with the other one. His fingers gently massaged one foot, kneading deeply into the soft soles. She had the prettiest feet, small and slender. Each toenail was impeccably manicured and painted.

She moaned, resting her head back against the over stuffed couch cushion. Her long black hair shone brightly against the camel-colored suede fabric.

"Daren, just when I thought you couldn't use those hands any better on me. Oh, that feels like heaven."

He didn't reply. There was no need. He had her exactly where he wanted her—under his spell and at his mercy. Tonight, he wasn't feeling so merciful with the little witch who wouldn't listen to her heart. If she thought for one second he'd accept that she declined his proposal, well, she was so very wrong. If he believed she truly wasn't interested, then he would not pursue it a second longer.

But what Cassandra had apparently forgotten was that Daren knew her better than she knew herself. He was out to prove it, by ensuring her complete sexual submission.

He smiled before raising her foot to his mouth and capturing her big toe in the warm wetness. His eyes remained on hers, tilting his head to see her.

She gasped, her head flung up. "What are you doing?"

He released her toe to talk. "If I must tell you, I'm sucking your pretty little toes."

"I can see that. Hell, I *feel* that. But what the hell for?"

He placed soft kisses along the small arch of her

foot. "Tell me you don't like it, baby. I'll stop."

"Well, oh, I didn't say that. Just, ah, didn't know you also had a foot fetish. Took me by surprise."

"I have a fetish about everything to do with you. Your feet, these slender legs, those luscious hips." His hand slowly slid up her body as he spoke against her foot. "Soft belly, voluptuous breasts, the pretty side of your neck. Your stubbornness. Your sarcasm."

He appreciated the flare of lust in her eyes as his fingernails gently scraped over her sensitive skin before he fisted her hair to draw her mouth to his. He abandoned her foot as his body moved over hers. His lips crushed against hers and his tongue traced the curve before she opened to let him taste her. The heady flavor of the wine remained on her tongue as he suckled it, licked the edge of it, and buried his tongue deep to take all of her breath.

"Delicious, Cass. I can't get enough of you," he whispered against her lips.

She whimpered, her palm flat against his chest as his weight pushed her deeper into the couch. His hand slipped under the T-shirt that she wore like a dress. It'd never looked that good on him. But since he helped her dress before dinner, he knew that was the only stitch of clothing on her body, the only obstacle to her nakedness.

"Daren. My wine glass," she said, desperately.

He'd forgotten she'd been holding it. When he leaned back enough to take it from her and place it next to his on the table, he noticed the red spot where it had splashed onto the shirt. Fuck it. He'd spill a gallon of it if it meant seeing her naked.

Slowly, because he wanted to seduce, even if he

tortured himself in the mean time, he moved his hands to where the hem of the shirt rested against her creamy thighs. Edging the material up revealed her beautiful skin inch by excruciating inch.

His cock strained against the fly of his shorts. With a snap of his wrist, he pulled the shirt over her head and had her in her birthday suit instantly. Well, Happy Birthday!

"Now your turn, Daren. Show me that magnificent body." She cringed. "I mean, please show me."

He smiled not caring if she remembered her submissive role or not. By the time he was through, she'd be his in every way and that would earn him her complete submission.

Quickly, he yanked his T-shirt over his head. He tossed it aside before standing to unzip his shorts and removing them with his briefs, while keeping his eyes glued to Cassandra. She watched him closely, that little tongue of hers darting out to lick at her lips. His cock sprang forward, relieved to be out of the confines of the shorts. It wanted badly to be fucking her mouth, but he reminded himself to go slowly.

He offered her his hand and tugged her up. From behind her, he grabbed the blanket off the top of the couch and led her to the fireplace. Strategically, he placed the blanket on the floor in front of the hearth so the heat from the flames wouldn't distract them.

After laying Cassandra on her back on the blanket, he retrieved their bag of sex store goodies. He'd make use of whatever he could to seduce her and drive her wild. Returning to her side, he noticed her eyes widen with excitement when she looked at his hand.

He removed the gold nipple clamps from their

packaging and knelt beside her. "Did you think I'd forget about all the sexy toys you picked out?"

Her smile was teasing.

His mouth covered her breast, sucking the nipple to a stiff peak. Moving back, he blew a long breath over it until he was sure it was as hard as it could be. Then he applied the same treatment to her other nipple. By now, she squirmed and moaned, her slender body moving like a snake in the grass.

"Are you ready to play, Cass?"

She nodded and bit her bottom lip. Didn't she look so fucking adorable? His cock flexed in agreement and begged for her pussy.

He drew in a long steadying breath, sure that he'd lose his mind before tonight was over. Cassandra was just too intoxicating for any sane man to walk away from unscarred.

Daren loosened the small clamp as her eyes fixated on his movements. Carefully, he lowered the clamp onto her erect nipple, tightening it into place. He paid close attention to her body language to gauge her comfort level. The clamps were meant to excite through a hint of pain, so it was his responsibility to know just where to draw that line. Her sharp intake of breath told him when. He dressed the other nipple in the same fashion. The sight of her clamped breasts joined by the thin gold chain made his dick salute.

"Are you comfortable, baby? Because you're so fucking hot right now. I'll be lucky not to come before I enter you."

She smiled, her hand moving to caress one of her secured nipples. "It's certainly interesting, a little painful, but highly erotic. I feel very naughty right

185

now."

"You're such a naughty little girl, I agree." He kept his eyes on her face, while his hands dug into the bag.

When he pulled out the thin wooden paddle, she gasped. The soft sound shot a fireball straight to his gut, tightening it painfully.

"Know what happens to naughty girls, Cass?"

She swallowed hard, her eyes as wide as he'd ever seen them. But she remained silent. That was a first.

He dragged the paddle along her arms and belly, down her thighs and legs. "They get their bare bottoms paddled. I've been wanting to paddle your sweet little ass for so long, baby. I'm going to take my time doing it."

Her breasts bounced up and down with her deep breaths, the pretty gold chain dancing across her creamy mounds. Dear God, he'd never wanted a woman so badly.

"Stand up," he ordered in his firm Dominant voice.

She quickly obeyed, jumping up to stand in front of him. When she trembled against his chest, it was all he could do not to skip the paddling and fuck her. But he had a plan and he'd stick to it if it killed him. Looking at Cassandra so aroused, there was a very good chance it just may kill him. Damn it, couldn't she see they were meant to be together?

Grabbing her elbow, he marched her to the arm of the couch. "Bend over. Hands on the cushion. I want to see that ass up in the air. Now."

"Um, okay." Her soft voice dripped with arousal.

When she was in position, he leaned down to her

ear. "Give me a word, Cass, that you want to use as your safe word."

"Safe word?"

"Yes. It's a word that's unusual and, if you speak it, will signal to me that you've had enough and I stop immediately. You should never do this kind of play without a safe word."

"Birthday. That's my safe word."

He smiled. She must be remembering her birthday spanking. Well, let's just see if he can live up to her memories.

"You're to remain exactly as you are. Understood?"

"Yes."

Her beautiful white ass cheeks stared back at him. Running his hand over them, he treasured the smoothness. Taking the paddle, he placed the cool wood against one cheek, leaving it there for a moment to add to her anticipation.

He raised it and snapped it down easily on her ass. She yelped, her body jiggling, the swing vibrating through her. He placed the paddle against the other cheek and whacked it gently. Another yelp. His hand caressed the pinkened cheeks. He could already feel her skin heating. His cock throbbed to get into that tight pussy.

Just a few more minutes of paddling her very fine ass. He didn't want to give her so much for her first paddling that she never wanted another. If he had his way, there'd be plenty of these erotic spankings in her future.

"Cass, baby, you okay?"

"Yes, fine. It's…um…different."

"That it is. But I'm not done paddling you. My compliments in picking out this sturdy instrument."

As he positioned himself to swing again, she groaned. The sound of the wood hitting her flesh snapped through the room followed by another yelp. With his foot, he swept her feet apart, wanting a view of that hot pussy. What he saw amazed him. Without a doubt, she was the woman for him. Her sweet pussy juices dripped from her swollen bare lips. Not able to resist, he swiped his finger through the soft folds of her pussy and was rewarded when she arched back but remained in position.

"Soon, baby. Soon I'll fuck you very well." *And soon you'll realize we're meant to be together.*

What he'd really like to do is paddle the stubbornness out of her, but since this was foreplay he had to keep his plan in mind. Cracking the paddle against each cheek four more times, giving a brief rest between, he finished the job, satisfied she'd enjoyed her very first paddling.

He gently rubbed her warm flesh, his body pulsating with need. "Cass, I wish you could see how beautiful your ass looks with this shade of pink."

"I think I can get the idea by the way it's stinging," she said, her tone sharp and edgy, her arousal confirmed.

When she went to stand, his hand moved to her lower back to keep her bent over. "Oh, no, baby. Stay right where you are. We're not through, yet."

"But I thought you were done paddling me?" Her question was filled with worry. He gave her praise for not shouting her safe word from the top of her lungs.

"That I am. But there's more pleasure in store for

that pretty little pussy before it gets my cock."

He quickly retrieved the bag and pulled out the vibrator, unwrapping it and popping in the batteries.

"Let's see how much you like your new vibrator, baby," he announced as Cassandra remained obediently draped over the arm of the couch

The light blue plastic slid easily into her slick pussy hole. When it was in deep, he turned the switch at the top and it hummed to life.

"Oh," Cassandra screeched and nearly shot off the couch. "Oh, my God, that feels good. Wow. Beats the hell out of my old vibrator."

He laughed, knowing she was indeed getting good attention since his fingers shook from the vibrations as he held the toy inside her. He leaned over her body, loving the feel of her silky back, her skin as soft as a cloud under his touch.

His mouth teased her ear, his lips nibbling on the delicate lobe. "Feel the rings on the vibrator, baby. Aren't they caressing your pussy walls like I said they would?"

"Oh, Daren. Oh. I can't take this."

"Yes you can, Cass. You have to until I decide you're ready for my cock."

"Birthday!" she yelled.

He laughed and nipped her ear again before moving to her neck. "You can't use your safe word now. You're not in any danger of being hurt or feeling pain."

"That thing is driving me crazy. Please. Oh, please, Daren, fuck me."

Ah, right where he wanted her. Needy. Horny. Almost his.

"I think I'll fuck you soon. Show you how wicked women are taught a lesson."

"Oh, Daren!"

"But just where will I fuck you? Your mouth? Your ass?" His fingers on the hand holding the vibrator toyed with the puckered opening of her anus. "Or your pussy?" His hand maneuvered the vibrator slowly in and out of the slick folds between her legs and he moaned. "Definitely fucking your pussy, baby. You're soaked."

"Then stop talking and show me what that big, bad cock can do. I need to feel you fuck me like never before, harder, faster. I want to hear us fuck. You know the sound I mean? The slapping of my flesh against yours?"

God, her mouth was so damn hot. He wondered if he'd created a monster by introducing her to kink or he'd just awakened a sleeping nymph.

"Giving the commands now are you, Cass?"

She whimpered, her voice showing she recognized her error. "Sorry."

"Good thing I enjoyed hearing how you want me to fuck you."

He quickly removed the toy, shut it off and tossed it on the couch. From his discarded shorts, he removed a condom and expertly sheathed his cock. He leaned over her, his cock at her pussy entrance. When he entered her, he did so in one thrust, her pussy taking the length of him without hesitation. Her wetness covered him as he plunged in and out, the sucking sound of his skin slapping against hers was what she wished to hear as his thighs smacked against her ass. She added her own sounds, soft moans growing into shrieks as he drove her closer to the edge, nearing her release.

His fingers dug bruisingly into her hips as he held her slender body steady, thrusting his cock into her so fast and hard he was afraid he'd hurt her. But she only offered him encouragement, begging him not to stop and demanding he go deeper, and, as if it were fucking possible, faster. Perspiration beaded over his hot skin. He didn't know what warmed him more, the fire at his back or the little fireball he held in his hands.

"Remember…the rules…Cass," he said, his breathing heavy.

"Rules? What rules?" she asked gasping.

"You can't come without my permission."

He expected her to raise hell and forget her submissive side especially after how she demanded to be fucked. So when her soft voice floated to his ears, her words were magical.

"Daren. If you would please allow me to come. I want your cock to be covered in my juices before you explode. So you see how much you pleasure me."

"Oh, Cass, baby. Come. Come now."

When she shattered under him, her shaking body collapsing onto the couch as her pussy tightened in a death grip around his cock, he imagined he'd lose his balls from the ferocity of his release. With his muscles trembling, he emptied the last of his semen into the thin latex, wishing it was her hot pussy instead. He fell across her back until he could catch his breath and confirm that he'd died and gone to heaven. He'd never felt like this before and was sure it had something to do with divine intervention. He'd never felt so connected to a woman, like she was his missing half and the air he breathed.

He'd set out to seduce Cassandra, but inadvertently tortured himself in the process. She hadn't declared her love to him like he'd hoped. She hadn't confessed her undying devotion like he wished to hear. Fuck! Why'd he have to fall in love with a woman who was bound to be the death of him either by fucking him to death or by breaking his heart?

Cassandra shifted restlessly under his body weight so he immediately climbed off her. He scooped an arm under her waist and lifted her into standing position. Turning her to face him, he first noticed her flushed skin. The gold clamps were still securely fastened to her rosy nipples, but he resisted giving the chain a little tug like it was meant for. He'd save that for the next time he got her to wear them, if there'd ever be a next time. He quickly unclamped both and laid his mouth over each nipple to soothe, sucking very gently and not trying to stimulate.

Cassandra was falling asleep on her feet. He scooped her up and carried her to the blanket, stepping away only to get another blanket before crawling in beside her. Just one look at her naked body, the sexy curves and soft skin, had his cock growing hard again. He had no use for a re-charged dick and, by the looks of the lovely woman lying beside him, neither did she. Unfolding the blanket, he covered them with it.

Tucking Cassandra under his arm, he spooned her, resting his face in the crook of her neck and listening to her soft breaths as she drifted deeper into sleep, while the fire dwindled in the fireplace.

"Sweet dreams, love," he whispered and drifted into his own slumber.

****

The next morning, Daren awoke to the heavenly scents of bacon and coffee, but no warm, naked Cassandra in his arms. He'd planned to slip his cock into her to awaken her with a good morning fuck, but it appeared she'd risen before him and spoiled his plans. For that, he'd just have to paddle her pretty little ass until she couldn't sit.

He didn't know at what point the fire in the hearth had extinguished last night, since he never felt the absence of the heat. Cassandra's warm body was all the warmth he needed. He could still smell her scent lingering in the room. The lilac fragrance mixed with vanilla would make him crave her whenever he smelled either. Which really sucked if he couldn't convince her to come to New Hampshire with him. He'd never be able to go into the creamery while they made the vanilla bean ice cream without thinking of her.

He stood and stretched before dressing in the briefs and shorts he'd discarded the night before. Just thinking about their lovemaking had his cock coming to life again. Painfully, he forced his semi-erect member into his shorts and zipped. He decided it best to hit the bathroom first and get rid of his cotton mouth before chasing the scent of breakfast. The smells were so mouthwatering, he made it to the kitchen in record time.

When he caught sight of the heaping plate piled high with eggs, bacon, hash browns and toast, Daren almost forgave Cassandra for waking before him and ruining his plans. Almost. While he still planned to paddle her gorgeous ass, he'd also make sure to kiss every inch of it, too.

"Morning you," she said after he stepped into the kitchen.

She still wore his T-shirt like she had the night before, making her the most adorable sight he'd ever seen so early in the day.

"This smells so good," he said, moving to take the coffee she poured and kissing her lips with a loud smack.

"I figured you worked up an appetite last night. It's the least I can do to help replenish some of your energy," she said, leaning her bottom against the counter, holding her coffee cup.

Shoving forkfuls of food into his mouth, he noticed her staring at him. He at least swallowed before attempting to speak. "I'm starving. Sorry. I'm eating like an animal."

"I think you do pretty much everything in an animalistic way," she said, offering a faint smile as she walked to the table.

That he couldn't argue with. "This was a pleasant surprise, but I had plans for you this morning."

She shot him a wary look from over the brim of her cup as she sipped. When she said nothing, he found it odd, but continued to enlighten her as to what she'd missed out on.

"I planned on slipping my cock deep inside that slick pussy of yours and waking you with a screaming orgasm."

"Guess it's my loss." Her abrupt tone was oddly out of place for the serene look on her face.

Now, a man knows when he's pissed off a woman.

Call it a sixth sense or just a self-defense mechanism, but when a woman looked sweet and calm but her voice dripped with hostility, then he knew better than to stick around. Maybe that was her plan. To chase him away. Not a chance in hell of that happening. So he did what any sane man in love would do. He asked the question that would offer him up for sacrifice, using his best smile as armor.

"Okay, Cass. Tell me what I did to piss you off."

"I didn't say I was pissed."

He looked at her cautiously. Whatever. Every instinct told him to be on guard.

She stood and stretched, the thin cotton material molding her breasts and highlighting the erect nipples underneath. "I'm going to jump in the shower, then I thought we could start for home."

Warning bells rang in his head. Oh oh. She wanted to leave early.

He studied her face, still no sign of anger. "Did I do something wrong, Cass?"

"No. Why would you think that?" she said casually as she stood looking down at him.

He placed his fork on his empty plate. "Then why leave first thing? We have all day to spend together. I have a lot more ways to convince you that you can't live without me."

He stood and moved to her, but she darted away from him, moving to the sink to wash her mug and his dish. So she was avoiding him.

He folded his arms and stood behind her. "Okay, spill it, Cass. Now. What's wrong?"

She shot him a quick glance over her shoulder before rinsing the cup under the water. "Nothing. I've had a great time, but I have to get home. I have things to do."

His jaw tightened as he told himself to stay calm. "Things? They're more important than making love with me? Or sitting with me and having a relaxing conversation on the beach?"

She turned to face him, drying her hands with a towel. Her eyes were darker now with a hint of temper in their depths. "Making love to you is at the top of my list, but we can't spend all day here when I have to get home, run errands, and get ready for the week ahead. And we can have that relaxing conversation on the ride home."

Trying his best to control his rising temper, he took a deep breath and reminded himself this was typical Cassandra. "Bullshit. You're trying to run from me."

She threw the towel onto the counter and crossed her arms under her breasts. "I am not. It just so happens that this weekend was a spur-of-the-moment plan, and, well, I had a lot of other stuff to do this weekend."

Okay, so she wanted to leave early. No big deal. He pulled her into his arms. Her head rested on his chest, but she felt stiff as a board.

"Have I convinced you to marry me, Cass?"

He didn't think it was possible, but she stiffened more and pushed away from him. Her eyes looked glassy, but he didn't dare mention it since she blinked furiously to keep the tears from falling. It broke his heart to see her like this.

"Us getting married is the craziest idea, Daren. You don't need to pretend to want to marry me any more. We've had great sex all weekend. I never expected anything more from you, so there's no need for this charade."

She could've slapped him in the face and it wouldn't have stung as much as her words. In fact, he would've preferred the slap to hearing her say his marriage proposal was a farce just to get her in bed. Fuck! How the hell had this gotten so damn fucked up? How would he ever convince this woman that she was his everything? Looking at her determined stare right now, the odds were against him.

He spoke slowly, intending to keep his hurt from showing. "Fine. Get showered and dressed. We'll leave in an hour." He grabbed her upper arms and hauled her up to her toes in front of him. "But damn it, Cass, some day you're going to have to stop pushing people away when they get close to you or you're gonna end up all alone." He dropped her back to her feet.

He stormed off, not caring if she was pissed at him now. He was right and she knew it. Goddamn stubborn woman was in love with him, her eyes admitted it. He felt it when they made love and she surrendered to him, and yet she wouldn't make the damn effort to build a life with him.

Home. She wanted to go home when they could explore this new level of their relationship. There was so much more that he wanted to show her now that they had explored and pleasured each other. He wanted to show her how much she meant to him, how much he cared about her. He needed to show her just how good it would be if she moved with him.

Fine. He'd bring her home. No fucking problem.

****

Cassandra packed quickly, brushing the tears from her eyes before they could slide down her cheeks. Of course she screwed this weekend up just like she knew she would. She hadn't missed the hurt in Daren's eyes when they argued. But what the hell did he want from her? Did he really expect her to believe he wanted forever after with her? Oh please! She only peaked his interest because she said no to his silly offer. He'd forget about her as soon as he bedded the next woman.

Her chest clenched painfully. She didn't want to think about Daren taking another woman to his bed no matter how inevitable it was.

She slammed the few clothes she had brought with her into the duffel bag and zipped it. A quick glance in the mirror assured her that she had concealed her tears well, her eyes weren't even red. She'd wear her sunglasses anyways.

When she got home, she'd do her best to carry on as usual. Maybe even after a few weeks Daren and her could salvage their friendship. She couldn't bear the thought of losing that on top of the disastrous end to the best weekend of her life.

Walking out to the kitchen, Cassandra found Daren waiting for her. Without a word, he took the bag from her and walked out to the driveway as she followed. When he opened her door, she dared to glance at him, his stare penetrating to her soul.

His eyes were menacing, the hint of temper in their depths. How dare he be angry? She plopped into the seat as he slammed the door and walked to his side. She should be the angry one for him trying to tease her with a fake proposal.

But one look at his profile and Cassandra had to admit that she may be terribly mistaken about his intentions. She'd never seen his jaw so taut, his face so hard, his composure so serious.

She sighed, put on her sunglasses, and laid her head back for the longest car ride of her life.

****

Daren made record time driving them home and didn't even get a speeding ticket. He would've welcomed the conversation with a cop since the mood in the car on the ride back was so gloomy and tense it was suffocating. They didn't speak. Didn't look at each other. Just existed for the car ride home.

When Daren walked Cassandra to her door, hauling her bags with him, he remained quiet.

"Daren, I'm sorry if I hurt you." Her voice was soft, sad.

If? If? He didn't respond, just waited for her to open her door so he could place her bags inside.

"I just can't give you what you want," her voice cracked.

He turned to face her. "Can't? Or won't? There's a big difference, Cassandra. And it doesn't change the fact that I love you. Always will."

He leaned down and kissed her hard on the mouth, intending to brand his taste on her lips. Pulling away, his eyes locked with hers for the longest moment of his life. He couldn't accept never waking up to this woman again, never seeing her skin flushed with pleasure, never feeling her pussy pulse over his hard cock. Never feeling her soft breath on his skin or hearing her laugh. He couldn't accept not having Cassandra and all her brilliance and stubbornness as part of his life.

Goddamn her stubbornness!

He threw his sunglasses on and stalked back to the car. Opening the driver's door, he stopped only to look at her one last time. Seeing her standing there, letting him walk away, crushed his heart. How he wished she'd run into his arms now. But he knew Cassandra and she wasn't about to do that or she wouldn't have let him get this far.

He drove off, leaving the woman he loved behind. He had to face the reality that he had absolutely no control over Cassandra's decision. He'd failed miserably at convincing her to marry him. Failed at breaking through her stubbornness. Failed at climbing the walls she'd surrounded her heart with.

He failed. Plain and simple. Failed.

Chapter Eight

The next day at work was a useless way to spend eight hours. Cassandra concentrated on absolutely nothing except her weekend with Daren. She had cried herself to sleep the night before, so her eyes ached and the headache she fought all day was stronger by the time she let herself into her apartment that evening.

Going straight to the medicine cabinet, she chugged two aspirin on her way to the living room. The roses Daren had given her for her birthday were still bright and beautiful, their fragrance noticeable as soon as she entered the room and a constant reminder of the man she loved.

Cassandra's fingers brushed over the silky red petal of one and her eyes watered, her heart breaking in two. "Oh God. What have I done?"

Her wish had come true—he loved her. And she ran. Why was she so damn afraid to take a risk for the one thing she'd longed for all her life? She knew why. She didn't want him to get bored of her like she feared he would. What would she do if one day Daren just decided to end their love affair and be done with her? And wasn't there basis for her fears? He hadn't called like she'd expected, no, hoped. Maybe he had second thoughts. And what if he did call? She didn't know what she'd say to him.

They could never go back to the way things were before they'd become lovers. How could they? Were they supposed to forget the intimate exploration of each other's bodies? Were they supposed to forget he'd asked her to marry him? Was she supposed to believe he really wanted to? Damn it! He'd made it clear they were just fuck buddies. Then he stunned her with an admission of love and marriage.

A lone tear streamed down her cheek.

Would it be so bad to take a chance with Daren? What did she have to lose? Everything was lost if she didn't take the chance. She'd always wonder what could've been for them.

Her phone rang to interrupt her thoughts. Looking at the caller ID, she recognized her sister's name. Just great. She didn't need this now.

"Hi, Sally." Her older sister only called when she needed Cassandra to do something.

"Cass, listen, Mom and Dad need you to pick up some things at the supermarket tonight. I have a book club meeting so I can't do it."

Typical.

Cassandra inhaled deeply and let out a long, satisfying sigh. "You know what, Sally? I can't."

"What?" her sister said, clearly shocked.

Cassandra never said no to her family, but things were about to change. It was time she thought of herself instead of wondering when someone in her family would need her to run an errand, arrange a repairman, go to a doctor appointment.

Cassandra's mouth fell open. "Oh my God."

"What is it, Cass?" Sally said from the other side.

"I've been a damn fool is what." She'd allowed her family to manipulate her all these years because she was the one who was single, free, with no commitments.

Well, she had a man who loved her now—she truly believed that Daren loved her—and damn it if she wasn't going to get him back. That is, if he'd still have her. Her heart broke at the possibility he wouldn't. She brushed her worries from her mind for now.

"Cass, I have book club and-"

"Then go to the store after book club or tell Dad to go himself. I'm busy. I've got to go."

"What? What's so important that it can't wait until you run to the store for Mom and Dad?" Sally demanded.

"My life," Cassandra answered simply and quietly hung up the phone.

She picked up the roses and walked into her bedroom. She placed the vase on the dresser across from her bed so they'd be the first thing she awoke to each morning.

They'd have to do for now. At least until she had Daren back in her bed and she awoke to see him first.

****

For the first time in a week, Cassandra was hopeful. She'd spent the entire miserable week crying, wracking her brain for how to get Daren back, and finally realized she was an idiot who needed to get her ass to New Hampshire. And fast!

With several suitcases packed, she crammed them into her car. She didn't know when she'd come back to get the rest of her things or if she would need to. There was always a chance Daren wouldn't want her any more. When she'd decided at three this morning that she'd move to New Hampshire to be with Daren, it had come as such a shock. To finally trust her heart and go to him had been the most important moment of her life.

She'd finally smartened up and realized she'd let the man she loved her whole life go because she was afraid he wouldn't want her forever. Of course he did. Daren never did anything without thinking it out. And he'd made it clear he wanted her. He'd asked her to marry him and now he was going to get the answer he deserved.

Now she'd enlist the help of Daren's father to find her way to him.

"Mr. Hughes? This is Cassandra Wright."

Over the other end of the phone, the old man bellowed, "Cassandra! I was hoping you'd be calling soon."

Now that confused the hell out of her. "You were?"

"Yes, my dear. You're calling for Daren's new address."

"Um, well, yes I am."

"Excellent. It's about time you two got together."

Her hand gripped the phone to keep from dropping it. "I'm sorry. Did you say Daren and I should get together? As in be a couple?"

"As in get married. That boy's been in love with you forever. I just don't think he realized it until I told him he had to move. Moving him away from you was the only way I could think of to get him off his ass and go after you."

"What? You mean you only promoted Daren to force him to marry?" She was totally stunned.

"Ain't no forcing that boy to do anything except what he wants to do. I needed someone for the New Hampshire site and he was bored in his position here. I knew he'd never leave you behind. Boy has more brains than that I'm proud to say."

She smiled at the compliment. "But he did leave me behind. He already moved."

"He's up there getting settled. Don't think for one second that he's not coming back for you. Of course, it'd make it a lot easier if you made it to him first. I believe he said something about hog tying you and hauling your stubborn behind back with him." He burst out laughing.

"Did he now?" She couldn't help but laugh with him.

"Here's where you'll find him." The elder Hughes rattled off the address as Cassandra's shaking fingers jotted it down legibly on the scrap of paper she wrestled from her pocketbook.

"Thank you, Mr. Hughes. And may I ask one more favor?"

"Of course. Anything for you, my dear."

"If you should happen to talk to Daren in the next few hours, please don't mention we spoke."

"Ah, a sneak attack," he said and chuckled.

"Not really. Just a surprise visit." Oh, he was going to be surprised that was for sure.

"Now, young lady. It'll be no visit once Daren gets a hold of you. Don't think that boy will ever let you go again."

She was hoping not.

"Thank you, Mr. Hughes," she said quickly and disconnected.

A few hours later, after breaking some speed limit laws and being reprimanded by two Massachusetts State Troopers, Cassandra continued on her way to Daren's office.

She used her cell phone to call his office. "Yes, this is Ms. Fry, the state health inspector," she told his secretary. "I'm afraid I need to schedule an urgent meeting with Daren Hughes."

"Mr. Hughes is here and will, of course, be available immediately upon your arrival. And when did you say that would be?"

Shit! She had no idea how much longer it'd take. "Let's say between now and the end of the day. My schedule is very busy, but I will be there. Please make sure he is."

"Absolutely. Actually he's coming out of his office right now. Why don't you speak to him? Please hold."

Oh, hell. Cassandra hit the disconnect button praying the secretary hadn't made note of her number if she had caller ID.

It didn't matter. She just wanted to make sure Daren was there. If she'd said it was her coming, he may have refused to see her no matter what his father said. She couldn't risk that so for now he'd have to worry there was a state inspector coming. If there was one thing to keep Daren in one spot it was a business responsibility.

Two hours later, when Cassandra pulled into the parking lot of Hughes Ice Cream, she was so happy to be out of her car after hitting terrible traffic. She took a deep breath and walked on wobbly legs to the front entrance, expecting Daren to run into her before she made it inside. But he was nowhere to be seen as she walked to the door clearly marked as the office.

The secretary showed Cassandra into Daren's office and promised to summon him right away.

Butterflies danced in Cassandra's belly as she walked nervously around the large empty office, unable to sit still, too eager to see the man she loved. To her relief, she didn't have to wait long.

The office door opened and she turned quickly to face Daren, who was decked out in dress pants, long-sleeve dress shirt, and tie. He was as gorgeous as ever, his sexy body so appealing she licked her lips.

His stunned expression proved he'd fallen for her little white lie. He hadn't expected her.

"Cassandra." Her name fell from his lips as his eyes sharpened and locked onto hers. "I'm sorry. This isn't a good time, baby. God, I wish it was. Can you give me an hour or two? I have an urgent appointment coming in."

"Would that be the meeting with the state health inspector?" she asked innocently.

"Yes. How would you know...wait a minute. You? You're my urgent appointment?"

She nodded. "Yes. I'm afraid so."

Relief covered his face. "Why didn't you just call and say you were coming?"

She shrugged, feeling a little foolish. "I wanted it to be a surprise. Plus, I didn't know if you'd agree to see me."

He moved to stand in front of her, his hands in his pockets and his head bent to look down into her eyes.

"Now why would I do something like that?"

"Oh, Daren. I was such a fool. I love you and I let you leave. Please tell me I haven't screwed up the best relationship I've ever had."

He grinned. "Well, that depends."

Her breath hitched and her nerves were on edge. "Depends? On what?"

His musky aftershave overwhelmed her senses as she committed the scent to memory.

"On what you're here for."

Her eyes searched the warm brown depths staring at her. "I'm here for you, Daren. I love you. I thought your marriage proposal was a spur-of-the-moment gesture and that you'd take it back once you realized what you'd asked."

"Should know me better than that, Cass. I don't do anything I don't want to."

She breathed deeply, her heart pounding. "I know, Daren. I was afraid to take a chance at something permanent with you, even though you're the only man I've ever wanted."

He removed his hands from his pockets and crossed his arms over that wide chest. "Are you here to stay, Cassandra? Because, so help me God, if you say this is just a visit I'm going to take you to my house, tie you to my bed, and never let you go."

She smiled, relief flooding her. "I was hoping you'd say that. I rather enjoyed our last encounter with bondage."

"Really?" When his lips brushed softly against hers, she felt the hesitance in his touch.

She sighed, long and hard, and relaxed. "Definitely. Daren, can you ever forgive me for almost walking away from you?"

His knuckles skimmed her cheek, sending a bolt of fire straight to her pussy. "I suppose I could paddle your pretty little ass until you can't sit for a week to teach you a good lesson. I really enjoyed using the paddle we bought."

"Oh, you do say."

His arms wrapped possessively around her and she welcomed his strength. "I do. And of course, a good paddling is in order for that blatant lie you concocted. Had my stomach in a knot all day thinking I had to face a health inspector hell bent on breaking my balls over some silly regulation."

Her bottom tingled in anticipation. "I guess I've earned my punishments, huh?"

"Yes, you sure have, baby. Maybe I'll also withhold sex for a while. That'll teach you."

She opened her mouth in shock. "You wouldn't dare."

He smiled wide. "No. Never. That'd be punishing myself. Instead, I'll just have to concentrate on thoroughly pleasuring you so you never walk away from me again."

Despite her best efforts, she sniffled quietly. "Oh, Daren, I'm so sorry. If you meant what you said about marrying me, I have an answer for you."

"Do you now? Okay. Then tell me, Cassandra Wright, will you marry me and make me the luckiest man in the world?"

Relief filled her heart. "Yes. As long as you'll still have me, that is."

"I was only giving you until tomorrow to come to your senses and realize we were meant to be together. I was headed back to Connecticut to handcuff you, and believe me I do have a pair, and drag you back here kicking and screaming if I had to, baby. We belong."

"I've missed your touch, Daren. I need you to make love to me. I'm burning up for you."

"You're not alone, baby. No hand job in the world could ever replace you. Believe me. I tried this past week. Just thinking of you made me so fucking horny. Come here."

He pulled her against his hard body and bent his head, his lips meeting hers. His tongue dove past her lips, plunging into her mouth, tasting her, devouring her. God, how she had missed his kisses, missed the taste of him.

****

Her sexy, slender body against his was a sight for his very sore eyes.

She'd come back to him. His Cassandra, who he loved more than life itself, had returned to him like he knew she would. Deep in his heart, he knew she'd come back. That fact was all that had gotten him through the last miserable week without her in his arms.

How many times had he laid awake trying to convince himself to tell his dad to screw this job? That his Cass was more important. But in Daren's heart, he'd known this was the best place for him and Cassandra. This is where they could begin their life together. Build a family. Build a legacy.

She broke the kiss. "Oh, Daren, don't let me go. Please. Never let me go. Please. Promise me. You have to promise me," she demanded, tears streaming down her face.

He gently brushed the wet drops from her cheeks until her skin was once again dry.

"I promise you, Cass, baby. I will never, ever, never, ever, let you go. You're mine. I'm yours. Forever. If you ever doubt that, I will seriously blister your ass. I love you with all my heart and could never live without you. This last week alone has been hell on me. I love you, Cassandra. Forever."

"I love you, Daren. Forever."

They stayed like that, entwined in each other's embrace for what seemed like eternity. But it felt so good.

"Thanks," Cassandra said softly against his chest.

"For what?" Daren asked, pulling her chin up to see her eyes.

"For making all my birthday wishes come true."

He laughed. "But you know, you're only allowed one wish per birthday."

Her smile electrified his blood. "I know. There's been a lot of birthdays since sixth grade. Thanks for finally making all those wishes come true. Think you can get away to show me that house of yours now?"

"Hell yes. That's the benefit of being in charge."

"Oh, and I do so like it when you're in charge. I've been a naughty girl letting you come here all by yourself." She placed her hand in his and let him lead the way.

"And as soon as we get to the house, I plan to show that very sexy body of yours what happens to my naughty girl when she denies me what I want."

"Show me what you got, big boy."

He laughed as he carried her off to the home and life he'd always hoped to share with her.

She wasn't the only one whose birthday wishes had finally come true.

Operation: Spank Me
Book I – Operation Series
By Christina James

Chapter One

3 months later

Spring had finally come to eastern Vermont after a long, grueling winter of blizzards and ice storms. As Emma Shields drove over the covered bridge that led to the middle of town, she inhaled the fresh warm air breezing through the open windows of her pickup truck. Wildflowers were springing to life, adding a fragrance to the air that chased away memories of the snow that had only recently melted. All the trees were budding and would be covered in green leaves within a few short weeks. The beautiful natural surroundings provided a pleasant backdrop to the unique shops, galleries, country stores, and family restaurants that crowded the center of town.

The residents of White Cap Creek, Emma's tiny hometown, were bustling about on this gorgeous Friday afternoon. The kids were out of school for the weekend, running and smiling. Mothers and grandmothers pushed strollers through the sunshine while window-shopping along busy Merridien Street, the only major thoroughfare throughout the small town. All other streets were narrow and quiet. But Merridien Street served a special purpose, a place where residents could converge and catch up on gossip and news-mostly gossip.

The older men smoked cigars and sipped coffee outside the Gin Mill Restaurant. It was nice to see the sidewalk patio open again for customers to enjoy their meals outside in the fresh air. Some sat with the newspaper, reading it front to back and everything in between. Afterward there would be some heated debates concerning world events. Some of the men raced to be the first to finish the daily crossword puzzle. Emma laughed at the routine of her small hometown. Most residents may not be up to date on today's technologies like computers and the Internet, but that stopped none of them from being informed citizens.

Emma swung her truck into a parking spot on the side of Galway Florist. Jumping out, she quickly removed her packages from the backseat and strolled into the shop. Mrs. Galway came out from the back as the front door chime signaled Emma's arrival.

"Emma. How nice to see you, dear," Mrs. Galway said, bustling her short, plump body to Emma's side to lean up on her toes and kiss Emma's cheek.

The woman was always pristinely dressed in blouse, long skirt, and shoes. Emma didn't miss the once over Mrs. Galway gave her as she walked into the room. Emma's choice of jeans and T-shirts was always a topic for discussion and she was grateful not to listen to another lecture on dressing like a woman or on the fine art of applying makeup. Emma worked on a farm for Christ's sake. Who was she to impress anyway? The horses?

"Same here, Mrs. Galway. Here are the roses you

ordered."

Emma carried the boxes of her prize roses to the back room for the older woman who followed closely behind.

"Oh, they smell so fresh and fragrant," Mrs. Galway announced, opening the boxes. "So beautiful, too. Your roses are just so exquisite."

"Thank you." Emma never tired of hearing compliments about her roses. Her hard work had paid off finally.

"Have some coffee, won't you?" Without waiting for an answer, Mrs. Galway poured a mug and handed it to her.

Emma automatically accepted the coffee with a stir of panic in her gut. She absolutely couldn't get stuck here talking to the well-meaning but nosy woman. She was too busy for small talk and gossip. "I can't, Mrs. Galway, but I do appreciate the offer. I have some other errands to do before heading home." To ensure she didn't get cornered, Emma talked while walking back to the front of the store, placing her coffee mug on the counter.

"Oh, I do worry about you being all alone out there on your farm."

Emma laughed, knowing that a typical match making session was in store for her if she didn't escape. "I'm just fine out there. There's nowhere else I'd like to be." *Except in Finn's arms.* Oh, hell. Where did that thought come from?

"You know, Emma. The Sanders' middle boy is looking mighty fine these days. Why just the other day I saw him hauling groceries for his mama. What a kind boy and educated. You'd do good to catch his eye. I could ask him to take you to dinner, if you'd like."

Embarrassment swamped Emma. Was she now so desperate that her neighbors thought she couldn't get a guy to ask her out without interference from them? Christ, she was twenty-nine-years old and could find her own man. Why did everyone think she needed a man? There was nothing wrong with living alone. She could do as she wished, come and go as she pleased. Hell, if she didn't want to make the bed then she didn't have to. And it was a bonus to have the house to herself, if she cleaned something then it stayed clean.

"That won't be necessary, but thank you, Mrs. Galway. I'm quite capable of making my own dinner arrangements. I'm just not interested." Emma relied solely on her manners when she really just wanted to scream at the constant matchmaking. Her objections always fall on deaf ears.

The older woman sighed, her pudgy fingers resting across her belly. "I figured you'd say no. Oh, well, back to business. I'll need two-dozen more roses for early tomorrow. Can you make it?"

"Promise not to have the Sanders boy here when I arrive?" Emma asked with a bit more sarcasm than she intended.

Mrs. Galway made a face acknowledging defeat. "Oh, very well. But I really do need the roses. Right before you came in, I got a special order. The young man was very adamant about having the most perfect roses." Mrs. Galway clapped her hands together with excitement. "Oh, he sounded so romantic. Odd that I couldn't place his voice though, and I know everyone in these parts. He had an accent I just couldn't place. And his voice was very handsome."

Emma didn't want to know how a voice could be handsome, so she didn't ask. A question like that would suck her into a lesson on romance for sure. "Didn't you ask for a name?"

"No, I didn't want to be nosy." Emma stifled a laugh while Mrs. Galway showed her the order form she had written the stranger's info on. "He just gave the initials MM."

Leave it to Mrs. Galway to find mystery in initials. "Guess that's better than nothing. I'll have the roses for you first thing tomorrow morning, Mrs. Galway. I do have to run now to finish my errands. I'll see you tomorrow."

When Emma was finally allowed to leave, she walked quickly to the General Store for a few quick supplies. While she usually enjoyed talking and mingling with her neighbors and enjoyed the adult company on her trips into town, she just wasn't in the mood today for small talk no matter how lonely she felt.

It had been over a week since she'd last talked to her pen pal, Finn, and she was worried about him. Stationed oversees in some God forsaken third-world country was part of his job as a military commander, but it still made her nervous when she didn't hear from him. And this had been the longest they'd gone without talking since they'd started writing each other.

The seven days since his last email had been long and worrisome. It was unusual for him not to write. Unusual not to get even a quick email. So to keep her mind occupied, Emma kept busy with errands and chores, always able to find something to do on her farm. It was funny how her life seemed so boring now that she corresponded with Finn and heard his tales of danger and adventure, not to mention all of the sexual things he wanted to do to her body. It wasn't that farm life was boring, because she loved every bit of it. But now, it felt as if her life was missing something.

"Emma, how are you?" Mr. Langston asked as he rang up her groceries while she daydreamed of military campaigns and what it would be like to risk her life every day as part of a job.

Shaking Finn from her thoughts, Emma cleared her throat before speaking. "Very well. How's Peggy? I miss seeing her around."

He let out a heavy sigh. "Decided to stay in Boston after college. Her mama's not happy, and neither am I, but we understand. Not many young people can live this quiet life we got going for ourselves around here. You're one of the few youngsters to stay here, Emma. Didn't you ever want to go anywhere else?" he asked, bagging her groceries as he tallied them on the old-fashioned keypunch register.

"Not really, Mr. Langston, and I'm not a youngster any more. I figure if I get the urge to see something else then I'll travel, but I can't think of anywhere else I'd rather live than White Cap Creek."

"Not gonna find yourself a fella around here since they're all moving to the city."

She laughed as another matchmaking session began. "Not looking for a fella, sir."

"Girl needs to have a man around the house. Don't you get lonely all the way out on that farm by yourself?"

This was the problem with living where you grew

up. Everyone knew your business. Especially in a small town like White Cap Creek. Privacy just wasn't really an option. "Not at all. I'm very busy with my roses and my horses." *And writing erotic emails to Finn.*

"Well, to each his own I suppose," he stated simply as he handed her the change with her receipt. "You have a nice day for yourself, you hear?"

She accepted the two brown paper bags he handed her. "Thank you. I will."

After finishing the last of her errands, Emma drove through town on her way home. Suddenly the charming scene that she had so much enjoyed on the ride in only made her sad now. It was obvious how happy the mothers pushing their strollers and the couples walking hand in hand were. The smiles on their faces said it all. Emma wanted a part of that. She just didn't know how to get it. And Mr. Langston was right. There were not many eligible men in White Cap Creek. The ones that were left were more than likely already planning to leave to chase careers that would take them away from what generations of families had helped build.

Emma Shields was no quitter but, damn, she felt like running from this town as fast as she could. That would make no sense since she'd only end up right back here. This was where her heart was even if her thoughts were oversees with a man she'd never meet.

****

Night fell silently around Emma's farm. The cool night air seemed a stark difference from the warm spring afternoon. Emma leaned against the porch railing, wrapped in her knit sweater, old T-shirt and jeans, and sipped a steaming mug of tea. Somewhere in the woods a creature made a shrieking noise. The sound wasn't scary, just something that went with the territory along with a thousand other noises that stirred the otherwise silent night. Looking out over her fields, Emma felt a sense of pride having kept the farm in her family.

Why wouldn't anyone want to live here? The air was fresh and clean. The weather was bearable and all four seasons paid a visit every year. Crime was practically non-existent. Neighbors were like family. But loneliness was abundant for those like her that lived farther away from the heartbeat of town. It had never bothered her before and she had a sneaking feeling why it was bothering her now.

Finn. He'd shown her what it was like to have constant male attention, even if it were only in the form of erotic emails. She closed her eyes and could almost feel his arms wrap around her and pull her against his hard body. She could almost feel the pleasures he promised. Could feel his warm breath against her neck, while his hands explored her body with exquisite caresses. She sighed for the lack of intimacy she yearned so much for. Craving something that much couldn't be healthy.

Her body hummed like a stick of dynamite waiting to ignite. The power was there, but only when the fuse was lit would it be useful otherwise it was just pent up energy. Fantasizing would surely drive her insane, but she loved how she felt when her imagination envisioned her in Finn's arms. How many times had he described just how he wanted to fuck her? He had promised to taste every inch of her skin, running his tongue along her body and leaving wet kisses in its path. The thought made her shudder with excitement. She pulled her sweater tighter around her. He made her hungry for him. Hungry for his damn touch.

No matter what they talked about, Emma wanted it all. Every position he'd described to her, how he'd bend her over and fuck her from behind, fuck her against the wall, spank her ass until it glowed. Oh God, when had a spanking ever turned her on? She had to admit that she fantasized about Finn's powerful arms holding her over his knees when she refused to send him pictures. She laughed because a spanking from Finn would be the ultimate sexual experience for her, being at his mercy, having him soothe her punished bottom, while whispering sweet words in her ear and holding her tight before he fucked her brains out.

Oh God, she needed to take the sweater off. Her body heated too quickly whenever she thought of Finn.

She looked up into the night sky dotted with stars and sighed, sadness consuming her as it had for the past few days. Where the hell was he? Why hadn't he gotten in touch with her? He had always emailed routinely, almost every day, if not a couple times a day with a few sentences to tell her he was thinking of her or what he was doing for work that day. It was natural for her to get used to that routine.

How she wished she had given him her phone number so he could call her like he wanted to. She longed to hear his voice. She already knew it'd be deep and strong. But she'd resisted because that would just make her little white lie even more complicated. It would just bring Finn closer to discovering the truth about her, that she was a fake.

Emma stomped back into the house and sat in front of her computer. Her heart sank, a dull ache settling into the middle of her chest when she clicked on her inbox. No new emails had arrived since she'd checked fifteen minutes ago.

No problem. If he didn't want to email her any more then that was fine with her. After all, he had never promised her anything but fantasy. A fantasy that she had chose to live in for far too long.

She no longer wanted his emails staring at her when she logged on, so she created a file and began transferring them. One particular email caught her eye and she couldn't help re-read it, remembering how it had changed their friendship from acquaintance to something neither of them knew how to explain.

My naughty Emma, oh the dreams I had of you last night. It took me an hour to fall asleep after reading how you would suck my cock. I swear I felt your mouth cover my dick as I read your words. My balls ached so badly. I closed my eyes and stroked until I shot my load onto my stomach, imagining how it would feel shooting my cum deep into your mouth. Watching as your little tongue lapped my cum from your lips. Do you know what you do to me you little tease? You drive me wild, so wild that I can't stop thinking about bending you over and entering that hot, slick pussy from behind. I want to feel my cock slide into your heat. Then I want to hear you scream my name, begging me to let you come. Would you come hard for me, Emma? I wonder how your juices will cover my cock as I thrust deep inside you. I dream of running my tongue through that bare pussy, licking at your sweetness collecting on your swollen lips. I want to taste you, baby. Oh hell yeah. I want to taste you over and over and over. Would you like that? Want to feel my tongue fuck that hot pussy? Sweet, sweet, Emma. I'm gonna spank you for making me crave you. That sweet little ass of yours will soon feel the sting of my hand and you'll love each spank. I promise. Think of me Emma. Want me like I want you. Sweet dreams, baby girl. Finn

Emma's body hummed in so many places that she shook. Logging off the laptop was the easy part. Walking to her bedroom was the hard part as her pussy throbbed with a need greater than she'd ever known. She stripped and dressed in her satin lilac nightgown. So what if she slept alone. Why couldn't she feel sexy while she dreamt of Finn?

She crawled under her blankets before opening her nightstand and removing her vibrator. Her heart was already pounding. Since she'd started IM'ing Finn and divulging her erotic desires, the slender pink plastic toy had gotten more use than ever before. She made sure to keep a decent amount of batteries in stock.

Closing her eyes, Emma sank onto her pillow, using her fingers to pull the edge of her nightgown up to her belly and imagining it was Finn's rough fingers baring her. Once she pulled her panties down far enough to access her clit, she envisioned Finn's hard body moving over hers like he promised. Her fingers gripped the long, slender vibrator, positioning it over her clit before turning it on. With the vibrations massaging her tender nub, she squeezed her eyes and gasped at the sensations rocking through her pussy.

225

The first touch of the wand was always the most sensual as it came in contact with her sensitive skin. The pulse from the wand's motion roared over her exposed clit, awakening even more need, and her hips automatically inched upward to meet the buzzing rod. Just the sound alone, the loud, constant humming, placed her senses on high alert. Her body knew what to expect as the vibrator edged closer to her pussy until it made contact with her clit and the need to come built with every second. The heavy ache deep within her pussy was never immediately alleviated by the first touch of the vibrator, as should be expected from such a powerful jolt on tender flesh.

The humming of the vibrator matched her ragged breaths, her body tensed, edged on by the sounds of pleasure. She concentrated on keeping the toy against her clit even as she wanted to yank it away, the sensation almost too much to bear as she awaited her release. She wasn't completely sure if an orgasm was even possible tonight. The building climax seemed more than she could handle as her mind begged for her to come. Is this how it would be with Finn? An all consuming mindless bliss?

Her juices flowed freely over her bare pussy lips, coating them in thin, slick moisture. That was also another luxury she had afforded herself since Finn entered her life. Even though she had to drive an hour to the closest day spa, Emma consistently kept her monthly appointment for an intimate waxing. It didn't matter that only she saw the results, but her soft, bare pussy lips made her feel feminine and sexy. In her mind, in her fantasies, Finn was enjoying the results as well.

Enduring thirty minutes of torture once a month as the hot wax was applied then ripped off to create the perfect Brazilian was well worth it. Those first hours while her abused skin healed, she would soothe herself with soft caresses over her bare mound. She imagined coming home to Finn kissing her pussy until she forgot all about the pain and only remembered the pleasure his mouth brought.

Emma angled the vibrator hard against her clit, causing her hips to buck, lifting her butt off the bed. The blankets had long since fallen off, and she sprawled half naked in the middle of her bed. Quick spasms rolled over her pussy lips like a roller coaster of pleasure. She could feel her explosion so close as she imagined Finn ramming his cock deep into her cunt, caressing her vaginal muscles and claiming her as his. Soon, he'd brand her with his hot seed as he emptied his release deep inside her heated pussy. It didn't matter that she'd only experience this wild intimacy in her fantasies, at least she had that much.

She gasped, tossed her head side to side, and fought against the rising urge to remove the vibrator from her clit, the intensity almost unbearable. Almost. This was one orgasm she needed more than air. Her body felt feverish, like flames surrounded her, bathing her in their heat until her skin glowed in a fine sheen of perspiration. Her nipples ached and begged for attention she couldn't give them, needing teeth clamping onto them, tugging them with gentle yet firm jerks.

Through one very descriptive email, Finn had taught her the fine art of how to pinch her nipples to mimic the way his teeth would tug on them so the pain blurred into pleasure, the pull on her nipples directly responsible for her pussy swelling in anticipation of a cock or dildo. Now, after months of erotic masturbation, her body was programmed to be greedy with every attempt at an orgasm. Her fingers or vibe may have worked her clit to reach orgasm, but every inch of her body was aware of the pleasure to come.

Holding the vibrating wand to her clit, Emma's hips shot off the bed again and she screamed, "Finn! Oh, Finn!"

The orgasm shattered her fragile control. Tremor after tremor snaked through her body, easing the tension in her pussy but building it in her heart. She yanked the wand away from her throbbing clit, the spasms gripping her pussy like fiery whips. What kind of fool fantasizes about a man she could never have? To Finn, she was a totally different woman, one made from lies of well-meaning friends. It was an image she couldn't live up to and one that Finn lusted over. Every one of her instincts had warned her about going along with such a devious scheme.

Disgusted with herself, Emma crawled from the bed, pulled her panties up, and adjusted her nightgown, the silk so smooth against her skin. She walked into the bathroom adjacent her bedroom and washed the vibrator then dried it.

One glance at her reflection in the mirror showed just how affected she was by her orgasm. Her face was flushed. Her lungs fought for air as she breathed deep to regain a normal rhythm. Her skin was damp with her efforts to reach orgasm. All thanks to one man at the center of her fantasies.

Walking back to her room, Emma tossed the

vibrator into the nightstand, climbed back into bed, and turned off the light.

With her pussy still pulsing from her orgasm and her body still warm, she kept the blankets off and snuggled into her over-stuffed pillow. Laying in her pretty nightgown, alone, Emma closed her eyes and dreamt of Finn, dreamt of a man who would forever only be a fantasy.

About the Author

Award winning, multi-published author Christina James lives in a Massachusetts suburb with her two children. When penning stories, she enjoys writing of romance and heartache and of characters who overcome the odds. Passion is at the heart of every tale, and she strives to create realistic characters, so the reader can fall in love with them as much as she does. A sucker for a good love story, Christina writes hot, sensual romances with a little sarcastic wit and some humor in a contemporary setting. Look for her naughty Operation Series to continue featuring the other Navy SEALs. For naughty and wicked romance with no strings attached…read a Christina James novel.

Other titles by Christina James:
A Place to Call Home
For the Love of a Woman
Operation: Spank Me
Operation: Tempt Me
Web of Lies

www.christinajamesauthor.com

Join Christina on Facebook
http://www.facebook.com/#!/profile.php?id=10000301
9022368&sk=wall